Polite Conversation

Polite Conversation

Jonathan Swift

ET REMOTISSIMA PROPE

Hesperus Classics

Hesperus Classics
Published by Hesperus Press Limited
4 Rickett Street, London SW6 1RU
www.hesperuspress.com

A Complete Collection of Polite and Ingenious Conversation first published in 1738
First published by Hesperus Press Limited, 2007

Foreword © Toby Litt, 2007

Designed and typeset by Fraser Muggeridge studio
Printed in Jordan by Jordan National Press

ISBN: 1-84391-147-7
ISBN13: 978-1-84391-147-0

CONTENTS

FOREWORD

I should probably begin by making some claim for the continuing relevance of Swift's *Polite Conversation* – that, for example, many of the banalities he catalogues are still in use today (keep your breath to cool your porridge; marry in haste, and repent at leisure; the more the merrier; the proof of the pudding is in the eating). I should insist that, essentially, genteel English discourse has not changed in the almost 270 years since Swift's book was first published. I should confidently assert that the modern-day equivalents of Colonel Atwit, Mr Neverout, Lady Smart and Miss Notable are still everywhere to be found.

But I can't.

Not because there isn't some truth in all these statements. But because what I feel, whilst eavesdropping on Swift's infuriating eighteenth-century talkers, is a sense of loss or, more accurately, of losing. This world is slipping finally out of range. I don't feel equipped with the right vocabulary, the right ears – and so what I am left with is something like the surreal inconsequence of a Shakespearean low-life scene. It is marvellous language, but it is now becoming language for language's sake.

That, at least, is how it is likely to be read in any edition without extensive notes to parse those phrases that have fallen totally out of use. These, though, are in the minority. Most of the time, the speaker's meaning can be figured out. And this quizzical kind of reading is one of the great pleasures, for me, of *Polite Conversation*.

My sense of loss, however, is also there in the world of Swift's words. The three Dialogues that, after the Introduction, make up the bulk of the book, take place, briefly, in St James's

Park and thereafter in Lady Smart's townhouse. Yet although smart and metropolitan in overall tone, the figurative language that comes up – particularly the old phrases and proverbs – bespeaks a recent rural past.

'Why everyone as they like, as the good woman said when she kiss'd her cow.' 'The parson always christens his own child first.' 'Come sit down on my lap; more sacks upon the mill.' 'The fox is the finder.'

There is a self-consciousness here. Many of the phrases are pitched so as to say, 'I am distanced from this, but have not completely lost touch.' The conversation is almost, at points, a version of the pastoral.

Other things, too, are being left behind. Religion, in this more free-thinking age, is no longer a matter of intense anxiety. Instead, as this exchange shows, there is sport to be had with people's faith:

LADY SMART: What religion is he of?

LD SPARKISH: Why he is an Anythingarian.

LADY ANSW: I believe he has his religion to choose, my Lord.

There are also, as in Shakespeare's *Henry IV* Parts I and II, frequent references to hanging. But they are less gnawingly anxious, because there is almost no chance that Mr Neverout will end up swinging, whereas the gallows is an occupational hazard for Nym, Bardolph, Pistol and Sir John Falstaff.

However, there is a huge amount here that comes through with great directness. As with most banal conversation, the main subjects are what is immediately present: the people in the room and the matter in hand – taking morning tea (Dialogue I), eating dinner (Dialogue II) and taking after-dinner tea (Dialogue III).

And a truly stupendous amount of eating goes on in Dialogue II. The feast includes oysters, sirloin of beef, shoulder of veal, fish, venison pasty, tongue, pigeon, fritters, soup, pullet, black pudding, almond pudding, ham, jelly, goose, bread, rabbit, partridge. And, to finish the meal off, 'A footman brings a great whole cheese'. These are creatures of appetite, living in an age when diet meant what you ate, not what you didn't eat. They are full of life – bitchy, snobbish, ribald, flirtatious, sarcastic and, occasionally, witty. They may no longer be our contemporaries, but we know them well enough. They are gluttons.

So far, I have managed not to mention satire. But in the face of such conspicuous consumption, it can no longer be avoided.

Swift's epitaph – my favourite ever – was to read, 'He has gone where savage indignation can no longer lacerate his heart.' Yet there is very little evidence of *saeva indignatio* in *Polite Conversation*. Swift doesn't despise any of his characters. Although of the ruling class, they are revealed as too powerless to bother about. Swift does not actively satirise them, merely allows them to blather inanely on until they've done the job themselves. In this context, *Polite Conversation* seems the obverse of Swift's *Directions to Servants*, where the tyranny of the below-stairs is clear from the beginning.

The satire of the Introduction, still gentle, is of a different sort. Here, Swift speaks in the person of Mr Simon Wagstaff, would-be purifier of the dialect of the tribe. What he offers the public is 'a thousand shining questions, answers, repartees, replies, and rejoinders, fitted to adorn every kind of discourse that an assembly of English ladies and gentlemen... can possibly want.' Wagstaff is in little doubt as to the importance of his work, both to his contemporaries and posterity:

I have been assured by more than one credible person how some of my enemies have industriously whispered about that one Isaac Newton, an instrument-maker, formerly living near Leicester-fields, and afterwards a workman in the Mint at the Tower, might possibly pretend to vie with me for fame in future times.

With this, the relationship between the satirist and the satirised comes into question. For Swift's ambitions were not all that different to Wagstaff's. Swift wrote for people's improvement (if you do not believe people can mend their ways, there is no point addressing them at all); his examples, however, were negative. 'Here,' Swift says, 'is what *not* to say.' A true solipsist would wish the whole human race to shut up. That is not the sense that *Polite Conversation* gives off. Swift is in such a holiday mood that he could almost be agreeing with Jane Austen's Mr Bennet: 'For what do we live, but to make sport for our neighbours, and laugh at them in our turn?'

Satire, to a certain extent, always loves its object; without its object, it would have no cause to exist – and the more loathsome the object, the more cause to exist. What truly intense satire feels, however, is *I hate it that I love this*. There is deep sorrow and shame beneath the fury. Mockery, which is all that most satire can aspire to, comes from a different motive: *I love it that I hate this. Polite Conversation* falls somewhere halfway between mockery and satire. Swift is hatefully in love with his loveably hateful speakers, and we are, too.

– *Toby Litt, 2007*

A COMPLETE COLLECTION OF GENTEEL AND INGENIOUS CONVERSATION

ACCORDING TO

THE MOST POLITE MODE AND METHOD NOW USED AT COURT

AND IN

THE BEST COMPANIES OF ENGLAND

IN THREE DIALOGUES

BY SIMON WAGSTAFF, Esq.

INTRODUCTION

As my life has been chiefly spent in consulting the honour and welfare of my country for more than forty years past, not without answerable success, if the world and my friends have not flattered me; so there is no point wherein I have so much laboured, as that of improving and polishing all parts of conversation between persons of quality, whether they meet by accident or invitation, at meals, tea, or visits, mornings, noon, or evenings.

I have passed, perhaps, more time than any other man of my age and country in visits and assemblies, where the polite persons of both sexes distinguish themselves; and could not without much grief observe how frequently both gentlemen and ladies are at a loss for questions, answers, replies, and rejoinders. However, my concern was much abated, when I found that these defects were not occasioned by any want of materials, but because those materials were not in every hand: for instance, one lady can give an answer better than ask a question, one gentleman is happy at a reply, another excels in a rejoinder; one can revive a languishing conversation by a sudden surprising sentence, another is more dexterous in seconding, a third can fill up the gap with laughing or commending what has been said: thus fresh hints may be started, and the ball of the discourse kept up.

But, alas! this is too seldom the case, even in the most select companies. How often do we see at court, at public visiting days, at great men's levees, and other places of general meeting, that the conversation falls and drops to nothing, like a fire without supply of fuel! This is what we all ought to lament, and against this dangerous evil I take upon me to affirm, that I have in the following papers provided an infallible remedy. It was in the year 1695, and the sixth of his late majesty King William the Third[1] of ever glorious and immortal memory, who rescued three kingdoms from popery and slavery, when, being about the age of six and thirty, my judgement mature, of good reputation in the world, and well acquainted with the best families in town, I determined to spend five mornings, to dine four times, pass three afternoons and six evenings every week in the houses of the most polite families, of which I would confine myself to fifty, only changing as the masters or ladies died, or left the town, or grew out of vogue, or sunk in their fortunes, or (which to me was of the highest moment) became disaffected to the government; which practice I have followed ever since to this very day, except when I happened to be sick, or in the spleen upon cloudy weather, and except when I entertained four of each sex at my own lodgings once in a month, by way of retaliation.

I always kept a large table book in my pocket, and as soon as I left the company I immediately entered the choicest expressions that passed during the visit; which, returning home, I transcribed in a fair hand, but somewhat enlarged; and had made the greatest part of my collection in twelve years, but not digested into any method, for this I found was a work of infinite labour, and what required the nicest judgement, and consequently could not be brought to any degree of perfection in less than sixteen years more.

Herein I resolved to exceed the advice of Horace, a Roman poet, which I have read in Mr Creech's admirable translation, that an author should keep his works nine years in his closet, before he ventured to publish them: and finding that I still received some additional flowers of wit and language, although in a very small number, I determined to defer the publication, to pursue my design, and exhaust, if possible, the whole

4

subject, that I might present a complete system to the world; for I am convinced, by long experience, that the critics will be as severe as their old envy against me can make them. I foresee they will object, that I have inserted many answers and replies that are neither witty, humorous, polite, nor authentic; and have omitted others that would have been highly useful, as well as entertaining. But let them come to particulars, and I will boldly engage to confute their malice.

For these last six or seven years I have not been able to add above nine valuable sentences to enrich my collection, from whence I conclude that what remains will amount only to a trifle. However, if, after the publication of this work, any lady or gentleman, when they have read it, shall find the least thing of importance omitted, I desire they will please to supply my defects by communicating to me their discoveries; and their letters may be directed to Simon Wagstaff, Esq., at his lodgings next door to the Gloucester Head in St James's Street, paying the postage. In return of which favour, I shall make honourable mention of their names in a short preface to the second edition.

In the meantime, I cannot but with some pride, and much pleasure, congratulate with my dear country, which has outdone all the nations of Europe in advancing the whole art of conversation to the greatest height it is capable of reaching; and therefore, being entirely convinced that the collection I now offer to the public is full and complete, I may at the same time boldly affirm, that the whole genius, humour, politeness, and eloquence of England, are summed up in it; nor is the treasure small, wherein are to be found at least a thousand shining questions, answers, repartees, replies, and rejoinders, fitted to adorn every kind of discourse that an assembly of English ladies and gentlemen, met together for their mutual entertainment, can possibly want, especially when the several flowers shall be set off and improved by the speakers, with every circumstance of preface and circumlocution, in proper terms, and attended with praise, laughter, or admiration.

There is a natural involuntary distortion of the muscles, which is the anatomical cause of laughter; but there is another cause of laughter that decency requires, and is the undoubted mark of a good taste, as well as of a polite, obliging behaviour; neither is this to be acquired without much observation, long practice, and sound judgement; I did, therefore, once intend, for the ease of the learner, to set down in all parts of the following dialogues, certain marks, asterisks, or *nota benes* (in English, markwells) after most questions, and every reply or answer; directing exactly the moment when one, two, or all the company are to laugh; but having duly considered that this expedient would too much enlarge the bulk of the volume, and consequently the price, and likewise that something ought to be left for ingenious readers to find out, I have determined to leave that whole affair, although of great importance, to their own discretion.

The reader must learn by all means to distinguish between proverbs and those polite speeches that beautify conversation; for as to the former, I utterly reject them out of all ingenious discourse. I acknowledge, indeed, that there may possibly be found in this treatise a few sayings, among so great a number of smart turns of wit and humour as I have produced, that have a proverbial air; however, I hope it will be considered that even these were not originally proverbs, but the genuine pro- ductions of superior wits, to embellish and support conversa- tion; whence, with great impropriety as well as plagiarism (if you will forgive a hard word) they have most injuriously been transferred into proverbial maxims; and, therefore, in justice ought to be resumed out of vulgar hands, to adorn the drawing rooms of princes, both male and female, the levees of great ministers, as well as the toilet and tea-table of the ladies.

I can faithfully assure the reader that there is not one single witty phrase in this whole collection that has not received the stamp and approbation of at least one hundred years, and how much longer it is hard to determine he may therefore be secure to find them all genuine, sterling, and authentic.

But, before this elaborate treatise can become of universal use and ornament to my native country, two points, which will require time and much application, are absolutely necessary.

For, first, whatever person would aspire to be completely witty, smart, humorous, and polite, must, by hard labour, be able to retain in his memory every single sentence contained in this work, so as never to be once at a loss in applying the right answers, questions, repartees, and the like, immediately, and without study or hesitation.

And, secondly, after a lady or gentleman has so well overcome this difficulty as never to be at a loss upon any emergency, the true management of every feature, and almost of every limb, is equally necessary; without which an infinite number of absurdities will inevitably ensue. For instance, there is hardly a polite sentence in the following dialogues that does not absolutely require some peculiar graceful motion in the eyes, or nose, or mouth, or forehead, or chin, or suitable toss of the head, with certain offices assigned to each hand; and in ladies, the whole exercise of the fan, fitted to the energy of every word they deliver; by no means omitting the various turns and cadence of the voice, the twistings, and movements, and different postures of the body, the several kinds and gradations of laughter, which the ladies must daily practise by the looking glass, and consult upon them with their waiting-maids.

My readers will soon observe what a great compass of real and useful knowledge this science includes; wherein, although nature assisted by genius may be very instrumental, yet a strong memory and constant application, together with example and precept, will be highly necessary. For these reasons I have often wished that certain male and female instructors perfectly versed in this science would set up schools for the instruction of young ladies and gentlemen therein.

I remember, about thirty years ago, there was a Bohemian woman of that species commonly known by the name of gipsies, who came over hither from France, and generally attended Isaac, the dancing master, when he was teaching his art to misses of quality; and while the young ladies were thus employed, the Bohemian, standing at some distance, but full in their sight, acted before them all proper airs, and heavings of the head, and motions of the hands, and twistings of the body; whereof you may still observe the good effects in several of our elder ladies.

After the same manner it were much to be desired that some expert gentlewoman gone to decay would set up public schools, wherein young girls of quality, or great fortunes, might first be taught to repeat this following system of conversation, which I have been at so much pains to compile; and then to adapt every feature of their countenances, every turn of their hands, every screwing of their bodies, every exercise of their fans, to the humour of the sentences they hear or deliver in conversation. But, above all, to instruct them in every species and degree of laughing in the proper seasons, at their own wit or that of the company. And if the sons of the nobility and gentry, instead of being sent to common schools, or put into the hands of tutors at home to learn nothing but words, were consigned to able instructors in the same art, I cannot find what use there could be of books, except in the hands of those who are to make learning their trade, which is below the dignity of persons born to titles or estates.

It would be another infinite advantage that, by cultivating this science, we should wholly avoid the vexations and impertinence of pedants, who affect to talk in a language not to be understood; and whenever a polite person offers accidentally to use any of their jargon terms, have the presumption to laugh at us for pronouncing those words in a genteeler manner. Whereas I do here affirm that, whenever any fine gentleman or lady condescends to let a hard word pass out of their mouths, every syllable is smoothed and polished in the passage; and it is a true mark of politeness both in writing and reading to vary the orthography as well as the sound; because we are infinitely better judges of what will please a distinguishing ear than those who call themselves scholars can possibly be; who, consequently, ought to correct their books, and manner of pronouncing by the authority of our example, from whose lips they proceed with infinitely more beauty and significancy.

But, in the meantime, until so great, so useful, and so necessary a design can be put in execution (which, considering the good disposition of our country at present, I shall not despair of living to see) let me recommend the following treatise, to be carried about as a pocket companion by all gentlemen and ladies when they are going to visit, or dine, or drink tea; or where they happen to pass the evening without cards, as I have sometimes known it to be the case upon disappointments or accidents unforeseen; desiring they would read their several parts in their chairs or coaches to prepare themselves for every kind of conversation that can possibly happen.

Although I have, in justice to my country, allowed the genius of our people to excel that of any other nation upon earth, and have confirmed this truth by an argument not to be controlled, I mean, by producing so great a number of witty sentences in the ensuing dialogues, all of undoubted authority, as well as of our own production, yet I must confess at the same time that we are wholly indebted for them to our ancestors; for as long as my memory reaches, I do not recollect one new phrase of importance to have been added, which defect in us moderns I take to have been occasioned by the introduction of cant words in the reign of King Charles the Second.[2] And those have so often varied that hardly one of them of above a year's standing is now intelligible, nor anywhere to be found, excepting a small number strewed here and there in the comedies, and other fantastic writings of that age.

The honourable Colonel James Graham,[3] my old friend and companion, did likewise toward the end of the same reign invent a set of words and phrases, which continued almost to the time of his death. But as these terms of art were adapted only to courts and politicians, and extended little further than among his particular acquaintance (of whom I had the honour to be one), they are now almost forgotten.

Nor did the late D. of R— and E. of E— succeed much better, although they proceeded no further than single words; whereof, except bite, bamboozle, and one or two more, the whole vocabulary is antiquated.

The same fate has already attended those other town wits, who furnish us with a great variety of new terms, which are annually changed, and those of the last season sunk in oblivion. Of these I was once favoured with a complete list by the Right Honourable the Lord and Lady H—, with which I made a considerable figure one summer in the country; but returning up to town in winter, and venturing to produce them again, I was partly hooted, and partly not understood.

The only invention of late years, which has anyway contributed toward politeness in discourse, is that of abbreviating or reducing words of many syllables into one by lopping off the rest. This refinement having begun about the time of the Revolution, I had some share in the honour of promoting it; and I observe, to my great satisfaction, that it makes daily advancements, and I hope in time will raise our language to the utmost perfection; although I must confess, to avoid obscurity, I have been very sparing of this ornament in the following dialogues.

But, as for phrases invented to cultivate conversation, I defy all the clubs of coffee-houses in this town to invent a new one equal in wit, humour, smartness, or politeness, to the very worst of my set; which clearly shows either that we are much degenerated, or that the whole stock of materials has been already employed. I would willingly hope, as I do confidently believe, the latter; because, having myself for several months racked my invention to enrich this treasure (if possible) with some additions of my own (which, however, should have been printed in a different character that I might not be charged with imposing upon the public), and having shown them to some judicious friends, they dealt very sincerely with me, all unanimously agreeing that mine were infinitely below the true old helps to discourse drawn up in my present collection, and confirmed their opinion with reasons, by which I was perfectly convinced as well as ashamed of my great presumption.

But I lately met a much stronger argument to confirm me in the same sentiments; for, as the great Bishop Burnet of Salisbury[4] informs us in the preface to his admirable *History of his own Times*, that he intended to employ himself in polishing it every day of his life (and indeed in its kind it is almost equally polished with this work of mine), so it has been my constant business for some years past to examine, with the utmost strictness, whether I could possibly find the smallest lapse in style or propriety through my whole collection, that, in emulation with the bishop, I might send it abroad as the most finished piece of the age.

It happened one day, as I was dining in good company of both sexes, and watching according to my custom for new materials wherewith to fill my pocketbook, I succeeded well enough till after dinner, when the ladies retired to their tea, and left us over a bottle of wine. But I found we were not able to furnish any more materials that were worth the pains of transcribing; for the discourse of the company was all degenerated into smart sayings of their own invention, and not of the true old standard; so that in absolute despair I withdrew, and went to attend the ladies at their tea, whence I did then conclude, and still continue to believe, either that wine does not inspire politeness, or that our sex is not able to support it without the company of women, who never fail to lead us into the right way, and there to keep us.

It much increases the value of these apophthegms, that unto them we owe the continuance of our language for at least a hundred years; neither is this to be wondered at, because, indeed, beside the smartness of the wit and fineness of the raillery, such is the propriety and energy of expression in them all, that they never can be changed, but to disadvantage, except in the circumstance of using abbreviations; which, however, I do not despair in due time to see introduced, having already met them at some of the choice companies in town.

Although this work be calculated for all persons of quality and fortune of both sexes, yet the reader may perceive that my particular view was to the officers of the army, the gentlemen of the inns of court, and of both the universities; to all courtiers, male and female, but principally to the maids of honour, of whom I have been personally acquainted with two and twenty sets, all excelling in this noble endowment; till, for some years past, I know not how, they came to degenerate into selling of bargains[5] and freethinking: not that I am against either of these entertainments at proper seasons in compliance with company, who may want a taste for more exalted discourse, whose memories may be short, who are too young to be perfect in their lessons, or (although it be hard to conceive) who have no inclination to read and learn my instructions. And besides, there is a strong temptation for court ladies to fall into the two amusements above mentioned, that they may avoid the censure of affecting singularity against the general current and fashion of all about them: but, however, no man will pretend to affirm that either bargains or blasphemy, which are the principal ornaments of freethinking, are so good a fund of polite discourse, as what is to be met with in my collection. For, as to bargains, few of them seem to be excellent in their kind, and have not much variety, because they all terminate in one single point; and to multiply them would require more invention than people have to spare. And as to blasphemy or freethinking, I have known some scrupulous persons of both sexes, who by a prejudiced education are afraid of sprites. I must, however, except the maids of honour, who have been fully convinced by a famous court chaplain, that there is no such place as Hell.

I cannot indeed controvert the lawfulness of freethinking, because it has been universally allowed that thought is free. But however, although it may afford a large field of matter, yet in my poor opinion it seems to contain very little of wit or humour, because it has not been ancient enough among us to furnish established authentic expressions, I mean such as must receive a sanction from the polite world before their authority can be allowed; neither was the art of blasphemy or freethinking invented by the court, or by persons of great quality, who, properly speaking, were patrons rather than inventors of it: but first brought in by the fanatic faction toward the end of their power, and after the Restoration carried to Whitehall, by the converted rompers with very good reason; because they knew that King Charles the Second, from a wrong education, occasioned by the troubles of his father, had time enough to observe that fanatic enthusiasm directly led to atheism, which agreed with the dissolute inclinations of his youth; and perhaps these principles were further cultivated in him by the French Huguenots, who have been often charged with spreading them among us: however, I cannot see where the necessity lies of introducing new and foreign topics for conversation, while we have so plentiful a stock of our own growth.

I have likewise, for some reasons of equal weight, been very sparing in double entendres: because they often put ladies upon affected constraints, and affected ignorance. In short, they break, or very much entangle, the thread of discourse; neither am I master of any rules to settle the disconcerted countenances of the females in such a juncture; I can therefore only allow innuendoes of this kind to be delivered in whispers, and only to young ladies under twenty, who being in honour obliged to blush, it may produce a new subject for discourse.

Perhaps the critics may accuse me of a defect in my following system of Polite Conversation; that there is one great ornament of discourse, whereof I have not produced a single example; which indeed I purposely omitted, for some reasons that I shall immediately offer, and, if those reasons will not satisfy the male part of my gentle readers, the defect may be applied in some manner by an appendix to the second edition, which appendix shall be printed by itself, and sold for six-pence stitched, and with a marble cover, that my readers may have no occasion to complain of being defrauded.

The defect I mean is, my not having inserted into the body of my book all the oaths now most in fashion for embellishing discourse; especially since it could give no offence to the clergy, who are seldom or never admitted to these polite assemblies. And it must be allowed, that oaths well chosen are not only very useful expletives to matter, but great ornaments of style.

What I shall here offer in my own defence upon this important article will, I hope, be some extenuation of my fault.

First, I reasoned with myself, that a just collection of oaths, repeated as often as the fashion requires, must have enlarged this volume at least to double the bulk; whereby it would not only double the charge, but likewise make the volume less commodious for pocket carriage.

Secondly, I have been assured by some judicious friends, that themselves have known certain ladies to take offence (whether seriously or not) at too great a profusion of cursing and swearing, even when that kind of ornament was not improperly introduced; which, I confess, did startle me not a little, having never observed the like in the compass of my own several acquaintance, at least for twenty years past. However, I was forced to submit to wiser judgements than my own.

Thirdly, as this most useful treatise is calculated for all future times, I considered, in this maturity of my age, how great a variety of oaths I have heard since I began to study the world, and to know men and manners. And here I found it to be true, what I have read in an ancient poet:

For nowadays men change their oaths,
As often as they change their clothes.[6]

In short, oaths are the children of fashion; they are in some sense almost annuals, like what I observed before of cant words; and I myself can remember about forty different sets. The old stock oaths, I am confident, do not amount to above forty-five, or fifty at most, but the way of mingling and compounding them is almost as various as that of the alphabet.

Sir John Perrot[7] was the first man of quality whom I find upon record to have sworn by *God's wounds*. He lived in the reign of Queen Elizabeth, and was supposed to be a natural son of Henry the Eighth, who might also probably have been his instructor. This oath indeed still continues, and is a stock oath to this day; so do several others that have kept their natural simplicity; but infinitely the greater number has been so frequently changed and dislocated, that if the inventors were now alive, they could hardly understand them.

Upon these considerations I began to apprehend that if I should insert all the oaths that are now current, my book would be out of vogue with the first change of fashion, and grow as useless as an old dictionary; whereas the case is quite otherwise with my collection of polite discourse; which, as before observed, has descended by tradition for at least a hundred years without any change in the phraseology. I therefore determined with myself to leave out the whole system of swearing; because both the male and female oaths are all perfectly well known and distinguished; new ones are easily learnt, and with a moderate share of discretion may be properly applied on every fit occasion. However, I must here upon this article of swearing most earnestly recommend to my male readers, that they would please a little to study variety.

For it is the opinion of our most refined swearers that the same oath or curse cannot consistently with true politeness be repeated above nine times in the same company, by the same person, and at one sitting.

I am far from desiring, or expecting, that all the polite and ingenious speeches contained in this work should, in the general conversation between ladies and gentlemen, come in so quick and so close as I have here delivered them. By no means; on the contrary, they ought to be husbanded better, and spread much thinner. Nor do I make the least question, but that, by a discreet and thrifty management, they may serve for the entertainment of a whole year to any person who does not make too long or too frequent visits in the same family. The flowers of wit, fancy, wisdom, humour, and politeness, scattered in this volume, amount to 1,074. Allowing then to every gentleman and lady thirty visiting families, not insisting upon fractions, there will want but a little of a hundred polite questions, answers, replies, rejoinders, repartees, and remarks, to be daily delivered fresh in every company for twelve solar months; and even this is a higher pitch of delicacy than the world insists on, or has reason to expect. But I am altogether for exalting this science to its utmost perfection.

It may be objected that the publication of my book, may, in a long course of time, prostitute this noble art to mean and vulgar people; but I answer, that it is not so easy an acquirement as a few ignorant pretenders may imagine. A footman can swear, but he cannot swear like a lord. He can swear as often; but can he swear with equal delicacy, propriety, and judgement? No, certainly, unless he be a lad of superior parts, of good memory, a diligent observer, one who has a skilful ear, some knowledge in music, and an exact taste; which hardly fall to the share of one in a thousand among that fraternity, in as high favour as they now stand with their ladies. Neither has one footman in six so fine a genius as to relish and apply these exalted sentences comprised in this volume, which I offer to the world. It is true, I cannot see that the same ill consequences would follow from the waiting woman, who, if she had been bred to read romances, may have some small subaltern or second-hand politeness; and if she constantly attends the tea, and be a good listener, may in some years make a tolerable figure, which I will serve perhaps to draw in the young chaplain, or the old steward. But alas! after all, how can she acquire those hundred graces, and motions and airs, the whole military management of the fan, the contortions of every muscular motion in the face, the risings and fallings, the quickness and slowness of the voice, with the several turns and cadences; the proper junctures of smiling and frowning, how often and how loud to laugh, when to gibe and when to flout, with all the other branches of doctrine and discipline above recited?

I am therefore not under the least apprehension that this art will ever be in danger of falling into common hands, which requires so much time, study, practice and genius, before it arrives at perfection, and therefore I must repeat my proposal for erecting public schools, provided with the best and ablest masters and mistresses, at the charge of the nation.

I have drawn this work into the form of a dialogue, after the pattern of other famous writers in history, law, politics, and most other arts and sciences, and I hope it will have the same success, for who can contest it to be of greater consequence to the happiness of these kingdoms than all human knowledge put together? Dialogue is held the best method of inculcating any part of knowledge, and I am confident that public schools will soon be founded for teaching wit and politeness, after my scheme, to young people of quality and fortune. I have determined next sessions to deliver a petition to the House of Lords, for an act of parliament to establish my book as the standard grammar in all the principal cities of the kingdom, where this art is to be taught by able masters, who are to be approved and recommended by me, which is no more than Lilly obtained only for teaching words in a language wholly useless.[8] Neither shall I be so far wanting to myself, as not to desire a patent, granted of course to all useful projectors; I mean, that I may have the sole profit of giving a licence to every school to read my grammar for fourteen years.

The reader cannot but observe what pains I have been at in polishing the style of my book to the greatest exactness; nor have I been less diligent in refining the orthography, by spelling the words in the very same manner as they are pronounced by the chief patterns of politeness at court, at levees, at assemblies, at playhouses, at the prime visiting-places, by young templars, and by gentlemen commoners of both universities, who have lived at least a twelvemonth in town, and kept the best company. Of these spellings the public will meet with many examples in the following book. For instance, *can't*, *han't*, *shan't*, *didn't*, *couldn't*, *wouldn't*, *isn't*, *en't*, with many more; beside several words that scholars pretend are derived from Greek and Latin, but now pared into a polite sound by ladies, officers of the army, courtiers, and templars, such as *jommetry*, for *geometry*, *vardi* for *verdict*, *lard* for *lord*, *learnen* for *learning*; together with some abbreviations exquisitely refined – as *pozz* for *positive*; *mobb* for *mobile*; *phizz* for *physiognomy*; *rep* for *reputation*; *plenipo* for *plenipotentiary*; *incog* for *incognito*; *hypps*, or *hippo* for *hypochondriacs*; *bam* for *bamboozle*; and *bamboozle* for *God knows what*; whereby much time is saved, and the high road to conversation cut short by many a mile.

I have, as it will be apparent, laboured very much, and I hope, with felicity enough, to make every character in the dialogue agreeable with itself to a degree, that whenever any judicious person shall read my book aloud for the entertainment and instruction of a select company, he need not so much as name the particular speakers, because all the persons throughout the several subjects of conversation strictly observe a different manner peculiar to their characters, which are of different kinds, but this I leave entirely to the prudent and impartial reader's discernment.

Perhaps the very manner of introducing the several points of wit and humour may not be less entertaining and instructing than the matter itself. In the latter I can pretend to little merit, because it entirely depends upon memory, and the happiness of having kept polite company; but the art of contriving that those speeches should be introduced naturally, as the most proper sentiments to be delivered upon so great a variety of subjects, I take to be a talent somewhat uncommon, and a labour that few people could hope to succeed in, unless they had a genius particularly turned that way, added to a sincere disinterested love of the public.

Although every curious question, smart answer, and witty reply, be little known to many people, yet there is not one single sentence in the whole collection, for which I cannot bring most authentic vouchers, whenever I shall be called; and even for some expressions, which to a few nice ears may perhaps appear somewhat gross. I can produce the stamp of authority from courts, chocolate-houses, theatres, assemblies, drawing-rooms, levees, card-meetings, balls and masquerades, from persons of both sexes, and of the highest titles next to royal. However, to say the truth, I have been very sparing in my quotations of such sentiments that seem to be over free, because when I began my collection, such kind of converse was almost in its infancy, till it was taken into the protection of my honoured patronesses at court, by whose countenance and sanction it has become a choice flower in the nosegay of wit and politeness.

Some will perhaps object that when I bring my company to dinner, I mention too great a variety of dishes, not always consistent with the art of cookery, or proper for the season of the year, and part of the first course mingled with the second, beside a failure in politeness by introducing a black pudding, I desire what would have become of that exquisite reason given by Miss Notable for not eating it; the world perhaps might have lost it for ever, and I should have been justly answerable for having left it out of my collection. I therefore cannot but hope that such hypercritical readers will please to consider, my business was to make so full and complete a body of refined sayings as compact as I could, only taking care to produce them in the most natural and probable manner, in order to allure my readers into the very substance and marrow of this most admirable and necessary art.

I am heartily sorry, and was much disappointed to find that so universal and polite an entertainment as cards has hitherto contributed very little to the enlargement of my work. I have sat by many hundred times with the utmost vigilance, and my table book ready, without being able, in eight hours, to gather matter for one single phrase in my book. But this I think may be easily accounted for by the turbulence and jostling of passions, upon the various and surprising turns, incidents, revolutions, and events of good and evil fortune, that arrive in the course of a long evening at play, the mind being wholly taken up, and the consequences of non-attention so fatal.

Play is supported upon the two great pillars of deliberation and action. The terms of art are few, prescribed by law and custom; no time allowed for digressions or trials of wit. Quadrille in particular bears some resemblance to a state of nature, which we are told is a state of war, wherein every woman is against every woman; the unions short, inconstant, and soon broke; the league made this minute without knowing the ally, and dissolved in the next. Thus, at the game of quadrille, female brains are always employed in stratagem, or their hands in action. Neither can I find that our art has gained much by the happy revival of masquerading among us, the whole dialogue in those meetings being summed up in one, sprightly, I confess, but single question, and as sprightly an answer. 'Do you know me?' 'Yes, I do.' And, 'Do you know me?' 'Yes, I do.' For this reason I did not think it proper to give my readers the trouble of introducing a masquerade, merely for the sake of a single question and a single answer; especially, when to perform this in a proper manner, I must have brought in a hundred persons together, of both sexes, dressed in fantastic habits for one minute, and dismiss them the next.

Neither is it reasonable to conceive that our science can be much improved by masquerades, where the wit of both sexes is altogether taken up in contriving singular and humorous disguises, and their thoughts entirely employed in bringing intrigues and assignations of gallantry to a happy conclusion.

The judicious reader will readily discover that I make Miss Notable my heroine, and Mr Thomas Neverout my hero. I have laboured both their characters with my utmost ability. It is into their mouths that I have put the liveliest questions, answers, repartees, and rejoinders, because my design was to propose them both as patterns for all young bachelors, and single ladies, to copy after. By which I hope very soon to see polite conversation flourish between both sexes, in a more consummate degree of perfection than these kingdoms have yet ever known.

I have drawn some lines of Sir John Linger's character, the Derbyshire Knight, on purpose to place it in counterview or contrast with that of the other company; wherein I can assure the reader, that I intended not the least reflection upon Derbyshire, the place of my nativity; but my intention was only to show the misfortune of those persons who have the disadvantage to be bred out of the circle of politeness, whereof I take the present limits to extend no further than London, and ten miles round; although others are pleased to confine it within the bills of mortality. If you compare the discourses of my gentlemen and ladies with those of Sir John, you will hardly conceive him to have been bred in the same climate, or under the same laws, language, religion, or government: and accordingly I have introduced him speaking in his own rude dialect, for no other reason than to teach my scholars how to avoid it.

The curious reader will observe that when conversation appears in danger to flag, which in some places I have artfully contrived, I took care to invent some sudden question, or turn of wit, to revive it; such as these that follow: 'What? I think here's a silent meeting! Come, madam, a penny for your thought'; with several others of the like sort. I have rejected all provincial or country turns of wit and fancy, because I am acquainted with very few, but indeed chiefly because I found them so much inferior to those at court, especially among the gentlemen ushers, the ladies of the bedchamber, and the maids of honour; I must also add the hither end of our noble metropolis.

When this happy art of polite conversing shall be thoroughly improved, good company will be no longer pestered with dull, dry, tedious storytellers, nor brangling disputers: for a right scholar of either sex in our science will perpetually interrupt them with some sudden surprising piece of wit that shall engage all the company in a loud laugh; and if, after a pause, the grave companion resumes his thread in the following manner: 'Well, but to go on with my story', new interruptions come from the left and the right, till he is forced to give over.

I have likewise made some few essays toward the selling of bargains, as well for instructing those who delight in that accomplishment, as in compliance with my female friends at court. However, I have transgressed a little in this point, by doing it in a manner somewhat more reserved than it is now practised at St James's. At the same time I can hardly allow this accomplishment to pass properly for a branch of that perfect polite conversation that makes the constituent subject of my treatise; and for this I have already given my reasons. I have likewise, for further caution, left a blank in the critical point of each bargain, which the sagacious reader may fill up in his own mind.

As to myself, I am proud to own that except some smattering in the French, I am what the pedants and scholars call a man wholly illiterate, that is to say, unlearned. But as to my own language, I shall not readily yield to many persons. I have read most of the plays and all the miscellany poems that have been published for twenty years past. I have read Mr Thomas Brown's[9] Works entire, and had the honour to be his intimate friend, who was universally allowed to be the greatest genius of his age,

Upon what foot I stand with the present chief reigning wits, their verses recommendatory, which they have commanded me to prefix before my book, will be more than a thousand witnesses: I am, and have been, likewise particularly acquainted with Mr Charles Gildon, Mr Ward, Mr Dennis, that admirable critic and poet, and several others.[10] Each of these eminent persons (I mean those who are still alive) have done me the honour to read this production five times over, with the strictest eye of friendly severity, and proposed some, although very few amendments, which I gratefully accepted, and do here publicly return my acknowledgment for so singular a favour.

And I cannot conceal, without ingratitude, the great assistance I have received from those two illustrious writers, Mr Ozell, and Captain Stevens.[11] These, and some others of distinguished eminence, in whose company I have passed so many agreeable hours, as they have been the great refiners of our language, so it has been my chief ambition to imitate them. Let the Popes, the Gays, the Arbuthnots, the Youngs,[12] and the rest of that snarling brood, burst with envy at the praises we receive from the court and kingdom.

But to return from this digression.

The reader will find that the following collection of polite expressions will easily incorporate with all subjects of genteel and fashionable life. Those that are proper for morning tea will be equally useful at the same entertainment in the afternoon, even in the same company, only by shifting the several questions, answers, and replies, into different hands; and such as are adapted to meals will indifferently serve for dinners or suppers, only distinguishing between daylight and candlelight. By this method no diligent person of a tolerable memory can ever be at a loss.

It has been my constant opinion that every man who is entrusted by nature with any useful talent of the mind is bound by all the ties of honour, and that justice which we all owe our country, to propose to himself some one illustrious action to be performed in his life, for the public emolument: and I freely confess that so grand, so important an enterprise as I have undertaken and executed to the best of my power, well deserved a much abler hand, as well as a liberal encouragement from the crown. However, I am bound so far to acquit myself, as to declare, that I have often and most earnestly entreated several of my above-named friends, universally allowed to be of the first rank in wit and politeness, that they would undertake a work so honourable to themselves, and so beneficial to the kingdom; but so great was their modesty, that they all thought fit to excuse themselves, and impose the task on me; yet in so obliging a manner, and attended with such compliments on my poor qualifications, that I dare not repeat. And at last their entreaties, or rather their commands, added to that inviolable love I bear to the land of my nativity, prevailed upon me to engage in so bold an attempt.

I may venture to affirm, without the least violation of modesty, that there is no man now alive, who has by many degrees so just pretensions as myself to the highest encouragement from the crown, the parliament and the ministry, toward bringing this work to due perfection. I have been assured that several great heroes of antiquity were worshipped as gods, upon the merit of having civilised a fierce and barbarous people. It is manifest I could have no other intentions; and I dare appeal to my very enemies, if such a treatise as mine had been published some years ago, and with as much success as I am confident this will meet, I mean, by turning the thoughts of the whole nobility and gentry to the study and practice of polite conversation; whether such mean stupid writers as the Craftsman,[13] and his abettors, could have been able to corrupt the principles of so many hundred thousand subjects, as, to the shame and grief of every whiggish, loyal, and true Protestant heart, it is too manifest they have done. For I desire the honest judicious reader to make one remark, that, after having exhausted the whole *in sickly pay-day** (if I may call it so) of politeness and refinement, and faithfully digested it into the following dialogues, there cannot be found one expression relating to politics; that the ministry is never mentioned, nor the word king about twice or thrice, and then only to the honour of his majesty; so very cautious were our wiser ancestors in forming rules for conversation, as never to give offence to crowned heads, nor interfere with party disputes in the state. And, indeed, although there seems to be a close resemblance between the two words politeness and politics, yet no ideas are more inconsistent in their natures. However, to avoid all appearance of disaffection, I have taken care to enforce loyalty by an invincible argument, drawn from the very fountain of this noble science, in the following short terms, that ought to be writ in gold, 'Must is for the king'; which uncontrollable maxim I took particular care of introducing in the first page of my book, thereby to instil early the best Protestant loyal notions into the minds of my readers. Neither is it merely my own private opinion that politeness is the firmest foundation upon which loyalty can be supported; for thus happily sings the divine Mr Tibbalds, or Theobalds,[14] in one of his birthday poems:

I am no scollard, but I am polite:
Therefore be sure I'm no Jacobite.

---

* This word is spelt by Latinists ENCYCLOPŒDIA, but the judicious author wisely prefers the polite reading before the pedantic. – H.

Hear likewise to the same purpose that great master of the whole poetic choir, our most illustrious laureate Mr Colley Cibber:[15]

Who in his talk can't speak a polite thing,
Will never loyal be to George our king.

I could produce many more shining passages out of our principal poets of both sexes to confirm this momentous truth. Whence I think it may be fairly concluded that whoever can most contribute toward propagating the science contained in the following sheets through the kingdoms of Great Britain and Ireland, may justly demand all the favour that the wisest court and most judicious senate are able to confer on the most deserving subject. I leave the application to my readers.

This is the work that I have been so hardy as to attempt, and without the least mercenary view. Neither do I doubt of succeeding to my full wish, except among the Tories and their abettors, who, being all Jacobites, and consequently Papists in their hearts, from a want of true taste or by strong affectation, may perhaps resolve not to read my book; choosing rather to deny themselves the pleasure and honour of shining in polite company among the principal geniuses of both sexes throughout the kingdom than adorn their minds with this noble art; and probably apprehending (as I confess nothing is more likely to happen) that a true spirit of loyalty to the Protestant succession should steal in along with it.

If my favourable and gentle readers could possibly conceive the perpetual watchings, the numberless toils, the frequent risings in the night to set down several ingenious sentences that I suddenly or accidentally recollected, and which, without my utmost vigilance had been irrevocably lost for ever; if they would consider with what in credible diligence I daily and nightly attended at those houses where persons of both sexes, and of the most distinguished merit, used to meet and display their talents; with what attention I listened to all their discourses, the better to retain them in my memory, and then at proper seasons withdrew unobserved to enter them in my table book, while the company little suspected what a noble work I had then in embryo; I say, if all these were known to the world, I think it would be no great presumption in me to expect, at a proper juncture, the public thanks of both Houses of Parliament for the service and honour I have done to the whole nation by my single pen.

Although I have never been once charged with the least tincture of vanity, the reader will, I hope, give me leave to put an easy question: What is become of all the King of Sweden's victories? where are the fruits of them at this day? or of what benefit will they be to posterity? Were not many of his greatest actions owing, at least in part, to fortune? were not all of them owing to the valour of his troops as much as to his own conduct? could he have conquered the Polish King, or the Czar of Muscovy, with his single arm? Far be it from me to envy or lessen the fame he has acquired; but, at the same time, I will venture to say without breach of modesty that I, who have alone with this right hand subdued barbarism, rudeness, and rusticity, who have established and fixed for ever the whole system of all true politeness and refinement in conversation, should think myself most inhumanly treated by my countrymen, and would accordingly resent it as the highest indignity, to be put on a level in point of fame in after ages with Charles the Twelfth, late King of Sweden.

And yet so incurable is the love of detraction, perhaps beyond what the charitable reader will easily believe, that

I have been assured by more than one credible person how some of my enemies have industriously whispered about that one Isaac Newton, an instrument-maker, formerly living near Leicester-fields, and afterwards a workman in the Mint at the Tower, might possibly pretend to vie with me for fame in future times. The man, it seems, was knighted for making sundials better than others of his trade, and was thought to be a conjuror, because he knew how to draw lines and circles upon a slate, which nobody could understand. But adieu to all noble attempts for endless renown, if the ghost of an obscure mechanic shall be raised up to enter into competition with me only for his skill in making pothooks and hangers with a pencil, which many thousand accomplished gentlemen and ladies can perform as well with pen and ink upon a piece of paper, and in a manner as little intelligible as those of Sir Isaac.

My most ingenious friend already mentioned, Mr Colley Cibber, who does so much honour to the laurel crown he deservedly wears (as he has often done to many imperial diadems placed on his head) was pleased to tell me that if my treatise was shaped into a comedy the representation performed to advantage on our theatre might very much contribute to the spreading of polite conversation among all persons of distinction through the whole kingdom. I own the thought was ingenious, and my friend's intention good, but I cannot agree to his proposal, for Mr Cibber himself allowed that, the subjects handled in my work being so numerous and extensive, it would be absolutely impossible for one, two, or even six comedies to contain them. Whence it will follow that many admirable and essential rules for polite conversation must be omitted.

And here let me do justice to my friend Mr Tibbalds, who plainly confessed before Mr Cibber himself that such a project, as it would be a great diminution to my honour, so it would intolerably mangle my scheme, and thereby destroy the principal end at which I aimed, to form a complete body or system of this most useful science in all its parts. And therefore Mr Tibbalds, whose judgement was never disputed, chose rather to fall in with my proposal mentioned before, of erecting public schools and seminaries all over the kingdom, to instruct the young people of both sexes in this art, according to my rules, and in the method that I have laid down.

I shall conclude this long but necessary introduction with a request, or indeed rather a just and reasonable demand, from all lords, ladies, and gentlemen, that, while they are entertaining and improving each other with those polite questions, answers, repartees, replies, and rejoinders, which I have with infinite labour, and close application, during the space of thirty-six years, been collecting for their service and improvement, they shall, as an instance of gratitude, on every proper occasion, quote my name after this or the like manner: 'Madam, as our Master Wagstaff says.' 'My Lord, as our friend Wagstaff has it.' I do likewise expect that all my pupils shall drink my health every day at dinner and supper during my life, and that they or their posterity shall continue the same ceremony to my not inglorious memory after my decease for ever.

A

COMPLETE COLLECTION OF POLITE
AND
INGENIOUS CONVERSATION

IN SEVERAL DIALOGUES

THE MEN   THE LADIES

Lord SPARKISH   Lady SMART
Lord SMART   Miss NOTABLE
Sir JOHN LINGER   Lady ANSWERALL
Mr NEVEROUT
Colonel ATWIT

ARGUMENT

Lord SPARKISH and Colonel ATWIT meet in the morning
upon the Mall; Mr NEVEROUT joins them; they all go to
breakfast at Lord SMART's. Their conversation over their tea,
after which they part; but my lord and the two gentlemen are
invited to dinner. Sir JOHN LINGER invited likewise, and
comes a little too late. The whole conversation at dinner; after
which the ladies retire to their tea. The conversation of the
ladies without the men, who are supposed to stay and drink
a bottle; but in some time go to the ladies and drink tea with
them. The conversation there. After which a party at quadrille
until three in the morning; but no conversation set down.
They all take leave, and go home.

Lord Sparkish *meeting* Col Atwit

Col: Well met, my lord.

Ld Sparkish: Thank ye, Colonel. A parson would have said, I hope we shall meet in heaven. When did you see Tom Neverout?

Col: He's just coming toward us. Talk of the devil –

Neverout *comes up*

Col: How do you do, Tom?

Neverout: Never the better for you.

Col: I hope you're never the worse; but pray where's your manners? Don't you see my Lord Sparkish?

Neverout: My lord, I beg your lordship's pardon.

Ld Sparkish: Tom, how is it that you can't see the wood for trees? What wind blew you hither?

Neverout: Why, my lord, it is an ill wind blows nobody good; for it gives me the honour of seeing your lordship.

Col: Tom, you must go with us to Lady Smart's to breakfast.

Neverout: Must! Why, Colonel, must's for the King.

[Col: *offering in jest to draw his sword.*]

Col: Have you spoke with all your friends?

Neverout: Colonel, as you're stout, be merciful.

Ld Sparkish: Come, agree, agree; the law's costly.

[Col: *taking his hand from his hilt.*]

Col: Well, Tom, you are never the worse man to be afraid of me. Come along.

Neverout: What! do you think I was born in a wood, to be afraid of an owl?

I'll wait on you. I hope Miss Notable will be there; egad she's very handsome, and has wit at will.

COL: Why everyone as they like, as the good woman said when she kiss'd her cow.

LORD SMART'S HOUSE;
they knock at the door; the porter comes out

LD SPARKISH: Pray, are you the porter?

PORTER: Yes, for want of a better.

LD SPARKISH: Is your lady at home?

PORTER: She was at home just now; but she's not gone out yet.

NEVEROUT: I warrant this rogue's tongue is well hung.

LADY SMART'S ANTECHAMBER

LADY SMART *and* LADY ANSWERALL *at the tea-table*

LADY SMART: My Lord, your lordship's most humble servant.

LD SPARKISH: Madam, you spoke too late; I was your Ladyship's before.

LADY SMART: O, Colonel, are you here?

COL: As sure as you're there, madam.

LADY SMART: O, Mr Neverout! What such a man alive!

NEVEROUT: Ay, madam, alive, and alive like to be, at your ladyship's service.

LADY SMART: Well, I'll get a knife, and nick it down that Mr Neverout came to our house. And pray what news, Mr Neverout?

NEVEROUT: Why, madam, Queen Elizabeth's dead.

LADY SMART: Well, Mr Neverout, I see you are no changeling.

MISS NOTABLE *comes in*

NEVEROUT: Miss, your slave; I hope your early rising will do you no harm. I find you are but just come out of the cloth market.

MISS: I always rise at eleven, whether it be day or not.

COL: Miss, I hope you are up for all day.

MISS: Yes, if I don't get a fall before night.

COL: Miss, I heard you were out of order; pray how are you now?

MISS: Pretty well, Colonel, I thank you.

COL: Pretty and well, miss! that's two very good things.

MISS: I mean I am better than I was.

NEVEROUT: Why, then, 'tis well you were sick.

MISS: What! Mr Neverout, you take me up before I'm down.

LADY SMART: Come let us leave off children's play, and go to pushpin.

MISS [*to* LADY SMART]: Pray, madam, give me some more sugar to my tea.

COL: Oh, miss, you must needs be very good humoured, you love sweet things so well.

NEVEROUT: Stir it up with the spoon, miss; for the deeper the sweeter.

LADY SMART: I assure you, miss, the colonel has made you a great compliment.

MISS: I am sorry for it; for I have heard say, complimenting is lying.

LADY SMART [*to* LORD SPARKISH]: My lord, methinks the sight of you is good for sore eyes; if we had known of your

coming, we would have strewn rushes for you: how has
your lordship done this long time?

COL: Faith, madam, he's better in health than in good
conditions.

LD SPARKISH: Well; I see there's no worse friend than one
brings from home with one; and I am not the first man
has carried a rod to whip himself.

NEVEROUT: Here's poor miss has not a word to throw at
a dog. Come, a penny for your thought.

MISS: It is not worth a farthing; for I was thinking of you.

COLONEL *rising up*

LADY SMART: Colonel, where are you going so soon? I hope
you did not come to fetch fire.

COL: Madam, I must needs go home for half an hour.

MISS: Why, Colonel, they say the devil's at home.

LADY ANSW: Well, but sit while you stay, 'tis as cheap sitting
as standing.

COL: No, madam, while I'm standing I'm going.

MISS: Nay, let him go; I promise him we won't tear his
clothes to hold him.

LADY SMART: I suppose, Colonel, we keep you from better
company, I mean only as to myself.

COL: Madam, I am all obedience.

COLONEL *sits down*

LADY SMART: Lord, miss, how can you drink your tea so
hot? sure your mouth's paved. How do you like this tea,
Colonel?

COL: Well enough, madam; but methinks it is a little moreish.

37

LADY SMART: Oh! Colonel, I understand you. Betty, bring the canister: I have but very little of this tea left, but I don't love to make two wants of one; want when I have it, and want when I have it not. He, he, he, he.

[*Laughs.*]

LADY ANSW [*to the maid*]: Why, sure Betty, you are bewitched, the cream is burnt too.

BETTY: Why, madam, the bishop has set his foot in it.

LADY SMART: Go, run, girl, and warm some fresh cream.

BETTY: Indeed, madam, there's none left; for the cat has eaten it all.

LADY SMART: I doubt it was a cat with two legs.

MISS: Colonel, don't you love bread and butter with your tea?

COL: Yes, in a morning, miss: for they say, butter is gold in a morning, silver at noon, but it is lead at night.

NEVEROUT: Miss, the weather is so hot, that my butter melts on my bread.

LADY ANSW: Why, butter, I've heard 'em say, is mad twice a year.

LD SPARKISH [*to the maid*]: Mrs Betty, how does your body politic?

COL: Fie, my lord, you'll make Mrs Betty blush.

LADY SMART: Blush! ay, blush like a blue dog.

NEVEROUT: Pray, Mrs Betty, are you not Tom Johnson's daughter?

BETTY: So my mother tells me, sir.

LD SPARKISH: But, Mrs Betty, I hear you are in love.

BETTY: My lord, I thank God, I hate nobody; I am in charity with all the world.

LADY SMART: Why, wench, I think thy tongue runs upon wheels this morning; how came you by that scratch upon your nose; have you been fighting with the cats?

COL [*to* MISS]: Miss, when will you be married?

MISS: One of these odd-come-shortly's,[16] Colonel.

NEVEROUT: Yes; they say the match is half made, the spark is willing, but miss is not.

MISS: I suppose the gentleman has got his own consent for it.

LADY ANSW: Pray, my lord, did you walk through the park in the rain?

LD SPARKISH: Yes, madam, we were neither sugar nor salt, we were not afraid the rain would melt us. He, he, he.

> [*Laugh.*]

COL: It rained and the sun shone at the same time.

NEVEROUT: Why, then the devil was beating his wife behind the door with a shoulder of mutton.

> [*Laugh.*]

COL: A blind man would be glad to see that.

LADY SMART: Mr Neverout, methinks you stand in your own light.

NEVEROUT: Ah! madam, I have done so all my life.

LD SPARKISH: I'm sure he sits in mine: Prithee, Tom, sit a little farther; I believe your father was no glazier.

LADY SMART: Miss, dear girl, fill me out a dish of tea, for I'm very lazy.

MISS *fills a dish of tea, sweetens it and then tastes it*

LADY SMART: What, miss, will you be my taster?

MISS: No, madam; but they say, 'tis an ill cook that can't lick her own fingers.

NEVEROUT: Pray, miss, fill me another.

MISS: Will you have it now, or stay till you get it?

LADY ANSW: But, Colonel, they say you went to court last night very drunk: nay, I'm told for certain, you had been among the Philistines; no wonder the cat winked, when both her eyes were out.

COL: Indeed, madam, that's a lie.

LADY ANSW: 'Tis better I should lie than you should lose your good manners: besides, I don't lie, I sit.

NEVEROUT: O faith, Colonel, you must own you had a drop in your eye; when I left you, you were half seas over.

LD SPARKISH: Well, I fear Lady Answerall can't live long, she has so much wit.

NEVEROUT: No; she can't live, that's certain; but she may linger thirty or forty years.

MISS: Live long! ay, longer than a cat or a dog, or a better thing.

LADY ANSW: Oh! miss, you must give your vardi[17] too!

LD SPARKISH: Miss, shall I fill you another dish of tea?

MISS: Indeed, my lord, I have drank enough.

LD SPARKISH: Come, it will do you more good than a month's fasting; here, take it.

MISS: No, I thank your lordship; enough's as good as a feast.

LD SPARKISH: Well; but if you always say so, you'll never be married.

LADY ANSW: Do, my lord, give her a dish; for, they say, maids will say no, and take it.

LD SPARKISH: Well; and I dare say, miss is a maid in thought, word, and deed.

NEVEROUT: I would not take my oath of that.

MISS: Pray, sir, speak for yourself.

LADY SMART: Fie, miss; they say maids should be seen, and not heard.

LADY ANSW: Good miss, stir the fire, that the tea-kettle may boil. You have done it very well; now it burns purely. Well, miss, you'll have a cheerful husband.

MISS: Indeed, your ladyship could have stirred it much better.

LADY ANSW: I know that very well, hussy; but, I won't keep a dog and bark myself.

NEVEROUT: What! you are sick, miss.

MISS: Not at all; for her ladyship meant you.

NEVEROUT: Oh! faith, miss, you are in lobs pound;[18] get out as you can.

MISS: I won't quarrel with my bread and butter for all that; I know when I'm well.

LADY ANSW: Well; but miss –

NEVEROUT: Ah! dear madam, let the matter fall; take pity on poor miss; don't throw water on a drowned rat.

MISS: Indeed, Mr Neverout, you should be cut for the simples[19] this morning: say a word more and you had as good eat your nails.

LD SPARKISH: Pray, miss, will you be so good as to favour us with a song?

MISS: Indeed, my lord, I can't; for I have a great cold.

COL: Oh! miss, they say all good singers have colds.

LD SPARKISH: Pray, madam, does not miss sing very well?

LADY ANSW: She sings, as one may say, my lord.

MISS: I hear Mr Neverout has a very good voice.

COL: Yes, Tom sings well, but his luck's naught.

NEVEROUT: Faith, Colonel, you hit yourself a devilish box on the ear.

COL: Miss, will you take a pinch of snuff?

MISS: No, Colonel, you must know that I never take snuff, but when I am angry.

LADY ANSW: Yes, yes, she can take snuff, but she has never a box to put it in.

MISS: Pray, Colonel, let me see that box.

Col: Madam, there's never a C upon it.

Miss: Maybe there is, Colonel.

Col: Ay, but May-bees don't fly now, miss.

Neverout: Colonel, why so hard upon poor miss? Don't set your wit against a child; miss, give me a blow, and I'll beat him.

Miss: So she prayed me to tell you.

Ld Sparkish: Pray, my Lady Smart, what kin are you to lord Pozz?

Lady Smart: Why his grandmother and mine had four elbows.

Lady Answ: Well, methinks here's a silent meeting. Come, miss, hold up your head, girl; there's money bid for you.

[Miss *starts*.]

Miss: Lord, madam, you frighten me out of my seven senses!

Ld Sparkish: Well, I must be going.

Lady Answ: I have seen hastier people than you stay all night.

Col [*to* Lady Smart]: Tom Neverout and I are to leap tomorrow for a guinea.

Miss: I believe, Colonel, Mr Neverout can leap at a crust better than you.

Neverout: Miss, your tongue runs before your wit; nothing can tame you but a husband.

Miss: Peace! I think I hear the church clock.

Neverout: Why you know, as the fool thinks –

Lady Smart: Mr Neverout, your handkerchief's fallen.

Miss: Let him set his foot on it, that it mayn't fly in his face.

Neverout: Well, miss –

Miss: Ay, ay, many a one says well that thinks ill.

Neverout: Well, miss, I'll think on this.

Miss: That's rhyme, if you take it in time.

NEVEROUT: What! I see you are a poet.

MISS: Yes; if I had but the wit to show it.

NEVEROUT: Miss, will you be so kind as to fill me a dish of tea?

MISS: Pray let your betters be served before you; I'm just going to fill one for myself; and, you know, the parson always christens his own child first.

NEVEROUT: But I saw you fill one just now for the colonel; well, I find kissing goes by favour.

MISS: But pray, Mr Neverout, what lady was that you were talking with in the side box last Tuesday?

NEVEROUT: Miss, can you keep a secret?

MISS: Yes, I can.

NEVEROUT: Well, miss, and so can I.

COL: Odd-so! I have cut my thumb with this cursed knife!

LADY ANSW: Ay; that was your mother's fault, because she only warned you not to cut your fingers.

LADY SMART: No, no; 'tis only fools cut their fingers, but wise folks cut their thumbs.

MISS: I'm sorry for it, but I can't cry.

COL: Don't you think miss is grown?

LADY ANSW: Ay, ill weeds grow apace.

A puff of smoke comes down the chimney

LADY ANSW: Lord, madam, does your ladyship's chimney smoke?

COL: No, madam; but they say smoke always pursues the fair, and your ladyship sat nearest.

LADY SMART: Madam, do you love bohea tea?

LADY ANSW: Why, madam, I must confess I do love it, but it does not love me.

MISS [*to* LADY SMART]: Indeed, madam, your ladyship is very sparing of your tea; I protest the last I took was no more than water bewitched.

COL: Pray, miss, if I may be so bold, what lover gave you that fine etui?

MISS: Don't you know? then keep counsel.

LADY ANSW: I'll tell you, Colonel, who gave it her: it was the best lover she will ever have while she lives, her own dear papa.

NEVEROUT: Methinks, miss, I don't much like the colour of that ribbon.

MISS: Why, then, Mr Neverout, do you see, if you don't much like it, you may look off it.

LD SPARKISH: I don't doubt, madam, but your ladyship has heard that Sir John Brisk has got an employment at court.

LADY SMART: Yes, yes; and I warrant he thinks himself no small fool now.

NEVEROUT: Yes, madam, I have heard some people take him for a wise man.

LADY SMART: Ay, ay; some are wise, and some are otherwise.

LADY ANSW: Do you know him, Mr Neverout?

NEVEROUT: Know him! ay, as well as the beggar knows his dish.

COL: Well; I can only say that he has better luck than honester folks; but pray, how came he to get this employment?

LD SPARKISH: Why, by chance, as the man killed the devil.

NEVEROUT: Why, miss, you are in a brown study; what's the matter? methinks you look like mumchance,[20] that was hanged for saying nothing.

MISS: I'd have you to know, I scorn your words.

NEVEROUT: Well; but scornful dogs will eat dirty puddings.

Miss: Well, my comfort is, your tongue is no slander. What, you would not have one be always on the high grin?

Neverout: Cry mapsticks,[21] madam; no offence I hope.

Lady Smart *breaks a teacup*

Lady Answ: Lord, madam, how came you to break your cup?

Lady Smart: I can't help it, if I would cry my eyes out.

Miss: Why sell it, madam, and buy a new one with some of the money.

Col: 'Tis a folly to cry for spilt milk.

Lady Smart: Why, if things did not break or wear out, how would tradesmen live?

Miss: Well, I am very sick, if anybody cared for it.

Neverout: Come then, miss, e'en make a die of it, and then we shall have a burying of our own.

Miss: The devil take you, Neverout, beside all small curses.

Lady Answ: Marry come up, what, plain Neverout! methinks you might have an M under your girdle, miss.

Lady Smart: Well, well, nought's never in danger; I warrant miss will spit in her hand and hold fast. Colonel, do you like this biscuit?

Col: I'm like all fools; I love everything that's good.

Lady Smart: Well, and isn't it pure good?

Col: 'Tis better than a worse.

Footman *brings the* Colonel *a letter*

Lady Answ: I suppose, Colonel, that's a billet-doux from your mistress.

Col: Egad, I don't know whence it comes; but whoe'er writ it, writes a hand like a foot.

MISS: Well, you may make a secret of it, but we can spell, and put together.

NEVEROUT: Miss, what spells b double uzzard?

MISS: Buzzard[22] in your teeth, Mr Neverout.

LADY SMART: Now you are up, Mr Neverout, will you do me the favour, to do me the kindness to take off the tea-kettle?

LD SPARKISH: I wonder what makes these bells ring.

LADY ANSW: Why, my lord, I suppose because they pull the ropes.

[*Here all laugh.*]

NEVEROUT *plays with a teacup*

MISS: Now a child would have cried half an hour before it would have found out such a pretty plaything.

LADY SMART: Well said, miss; I vow, Mr Neverout, the girl is too hard for you.

NEVEROUT: Ay, miss will say anything but her prayers, and those she whistles.

MISS: Pray, Colonel, make me a present of that pretty penknife.

LD SPARKISH: Ay, miss, catch him at that, and hang him.

COL: Not for the world, dear miss, it will cut love.

LD SPARKISH: Colonel, you shall be married first, I was going to say that.

LADY SMART: Well, but for all that, I can tell who is a great admirer of miss, pray, miss, how do you like Mr Spruce? I swear, I have often seen him cast a sheep's eye out of a calf's head at you: deny it if you can.

MISS: O, madam; all the world knows that Mr Spruce is a general lover.

COL: Come, miss, 'tis too true to make a jest on.

[MISS *blushes.*]

LADY ANSW: Well, however, blushing is some sign of grace.

NEVEROUT: Miss says nothing; but I warrant she pays it off with thinking.

MISS: Well, ladies and gentlemen, you are pleased to divert yourselves; but, as I hope to be saved, there's nothing in it.

LADY ANSW: Touch a galled horse, and he'll wince; love will creep where it dare not go; I'd hold a hundred pound, Mr Neverout was the inventor of that story; and, Colonel, I doubt you had a finger in the pie.

LADY ANSW: But, Colonel, you forgot to salute miss when you came in; she said you had not been here a long time.

MISS: Fie, madam; I vow, Colonel, I said no such thing; I wonder at your ladyship!

COL: Miss, I beg your pardon –

Goes to salute her: she struggles a little

MISS: Well, I'd rather give a knave a kiss for once than be troubled with him: but, upon my word, you are more bold than welcome.

LADY SMART: Fie, fie, miss! for shame of the world, and speech of good people.

NEVEROUT *to* MISS, *who is cooking her tea and bread and butter*

NEVEROUT: Come, come, miss, make much of nought; good folks are scarce.

MISS: What! and you must come in with your two eggs a penny, and three of them rotten.

COL [*to* LD SPARKISH]: But, my Lord, I forgot to ask you, how you like my new clothes?

Ld Sparkish: Why, very well, Colonel; only, to deal plainly
with you, methinks the worst piece is in the middle.

[*Here a loud laugh often repeated.*]

Col: My Lord, you are too severe on your friends.

Miss: Mr Neverout, I'm hot, are you a sot?

Neverout: Miss, I'm cold, are you a scold? take you that.

Lady Smart: I confess that was home. I find, Mr Neverout,
you won't give your head for the washing, as they say.

Miss: O! he's a sore man where the skin's off. I see Mr
Neverout has a mind to sharpen the edge of his wit on the
whetstone of my ignorance.

Ld Sparkish: Faith, Tom, you are struck! I never heard
a better thing.

Neverout: Pray, miss, give me leave to scratch you for that
fine speech.

Miss: Pox on your picture, it cost me a groat the drawing.

Neverout [*to* Lady Smart]: 'Sbuds,[23] madam, I have
burnt my hand with your plaguy tea-kettle.

Lady Smart: Why, then, Mr Neverout, you must say,
God save the King.

Neverout: Did you ever see the like?

Miss: Never but once, at a wedding.

Col: Pray, miss, how old are you?

Miss: Why I am as old as my tongue, and a little older than
my teeth.

Ld Sparkish [*to* Lady Answ]: Pray, madam, is Miss Buxom
married? I hear 'tis all over the town.

Lady Answ: My Lord, she's either married, or worse.

Col: If she ben't married, at least she's lustily promised.
But, is it certain that Sir John Blunderbuss is dead at last?

Ld Sparkish: Yes, or else he's sadly wronged, for they have
buried him.

MISS: Why, if he be dead, he'll eat no more bread.

COL: But, is he really dead?

LADY ANSW: Yes, Colonel, as sure as you're alive –

COL: They say he was an honest man.

LADY ANSW: Yes, with good looking to.

MISS feels a pimple on her face

MISS: Lord! I think my goodness is coming out. Madam, will your ladyship please to lend me a patch?

NEVEROUT: Miss, if you are a maid, put your hand upon your spot.

MISS: There –

> [*Covering her face with both her hands.*]

LADY SMART: Well, thou art a mad girl.

> [*Gives her a tap.*]

MISS: Lord, madam, is that a blow to give a child?

*LADY SMART lets fall her handkerchief,
and the COLONEL stoops for it.*

LADY SMART: Colonel, you shall have a better office.

COL: O, madam, I can't have a better than to serve your ladyship.

COL [*to* LADY SPARKISH]: Madam, has your Ladyship read the new play, written by a lord? It is called 'Love in a Hollow Tree'.

LADY SPARKISH. No, Colonel.

COL: Why, then, your Ladyship has one pleasure to come.

MISS sighs

NEVEROUT: Pray, miss, why do you sigh?

MISS: To make a fool ask, and you are the first.

NEVEROUT: Why, miss, I find there is nothing but a bit and a blow with you.

LADY ANSW: Why you must know, miss is in love.

MISS: I wish my head may never ache till that day.

LD SPARKISH: Come, miss, never sigh, but send for him.

LADY SMART *and* LADY ANSWERALL [*speaking together*]: If he be hanged he'll come hopping, and if he be drowned he'll come dropping.

MISS: Well, I swear you will make one die with laughing.

MISS *plays with a teacup,*
and NEVEROUT *plays with another*

NEVEROUT: Well, I see one fool makes many.

MISS: And you are the greatest fool of any.

NEVEROUT: Pray, miss, will you be so kind to tie this string for me with your fair hands? It will go all in your day's work.

MISS: Marry, come up, indeed; tie it yourself, you have as many hands as I; your man's man will have a fine office truly; come pray stand out of my spitting-place.

NEVEROUT: Well, but, miss, don't be angry.

MISS: No; I was never angry in my life but once, and then nobody cared for it; so I resolved never to be angry again.

NEVEROUT: Well, but if you'll tie it, you shall never know what I'll do for you.

MISS: So I suppose, truly.

NEVEROUT: Well, but I'll make you a fine present one of these days.

MISS: Ay, when the devil's blind, and his eyes are not sore yet.

NEVEROUT: No, miss, I'll send it to you tomorrow.

Miss: Well, well, tomorrow's a new day; but I suppose you mean tomorrow come never.

Neverout: Oh! 'tis the prettiest thing, I assure you; there came but two of them over in three ships.

Miss: Would I could not see it, quoth blind Hugh. But why did you not bring me a present of snuff this morning?

Neverout: Because, miss, you never asked me, and 'tis an ill dog that's not worth whistling for.

Ld Sparkish [*to* Lady Answ]: Pray, madam, how came your ladyship last Thursday to go to that odious puppet show?

Col: Why, to be sure, her ladyship went to see and to be seen.

Lady Answ: You have made a fine speech, Colonel; pray, what will you take for your mouthpiece?

Ld Sparkish: Take that, Colonel; but pray, madam, was my Lady Snuff there? They say she's extremely handsome.

Lady Smart: They must not see with my eyes that think so.

Neverout: She may pass muster well enough.

Lady Answ: Pray, how old do you take her to be?

Col: Why, about five- or six-and-twenty.

Miss: I swear she's no chicken; she's on the wrong side of thirty if she be a day.

Lady Answ: Depend upon it, she'll never see five-and-thirty and a bit to spare.

Col: Why, they say she's one of the chief toasts in town.

Lady Smart: Ay, when all the rest are out of it.

Miss: Well, I wouldn't be as sick as she's proud for all the world.

Lady Answ: She looks as if butter wouldn't melt in her mouth; but I warrant, cheese won't choke her.

Neverout: I hear my Lord What d'ye call him is courting her.

LADY SPARKISH. What lord d'ye mean, Tom?

MISS: Why, my lord, I suppose Mr Neverout means the lord of the Lord knows what.

COL: They say she dances very fine.

LADY ANSW: She did, but I doubt her dancing days are over.

COL: I can't pardon her for her rudeness to me.

LADY SMART: Well, but you must forget and forgive.

Footman comes in

LADY SMART: Did you call Betty?

FOOTMAN: She's coming, madam.

LADY SMART: Coming! ay, so is Christmas.

BETTY *comes in*

LADY SMART: Come, get ready my things. Where has the wench been these three hours?

BETTY: Madam, I can't go faster than my legs will carry me.

LADY SMART: Ay, thou hast a head, and so has a pin. But, my lord, all the town has it that Miss Caper is to be married to Sir Peter Giball; one thing is certain, that she has promised to have him.

LD SPARKISH: Why, madam, you know, promises are either broken or kept.

LADY ANSW: I beg your pardon, my lord, promises and piecrust are made to be broken.

LADY SMART: Nay, I had it from my Lady Carrylie's own mouth. I tell you my tale and my tale's author; if it be a lie, you had it as cheap as I.

LADY ANSW: She and I had some words last Sunday at church; but I think I gave her her own.

LADY SMART: Her tongue runs like the clapper of a mill; she talks enough for herself and all the company.

NEVEROUT: And yet she simpers like a furmety kettle.

MISS *looking in a glass*

MISS: Lord, how my head is dressed today!

COL: Oh, madam! a good face needs no band.

MISS: No; and a bad one deserves none.

COL: Pray, miss, where is your old acquaintance, Mrs Wayward?

MISS: Why, where should she be? you must needs know; she's in her skin.

COL: I can answer that; what if you were as far as she's in? –

MISS: Well, I promised to go this evening to Hyde Park on the water; but I protest I'm half afraid.

NEVEROUT: Never fear, miss; you have the old proverb on your side, Nought's ne'er in danger.

COL: Why, miss, let Tom Neverout wait on you, and then I warrant, you'll be as safe as a thief in a mill; for you know, he that's born to be hanged will never be drowned.

NEVEROUT: Thank you, Colonel, for your good word; but 'faith, if ever I hang, it shall be about a fair lady's neck.

LADY SMART: Who's there? Bid the children be quiet, and not laugh so loud.

LADY ANSW: Oh! madam, let 'em laugh, they'll ne'er laugh younger.

NEVEROUT: Miss, I'll tell you a secret, if you'll promise never to tell it again.

MISS: No, to be sure; I'll tell it to nobody but friends and strangers.

NEVEROUT: Why then, there's some dirt in my teacup.

Miss: Come, come, the more there's in't the more there's on't.

Lady Answ: Poh! you must eat a peck of dirt before you die.

Col: Ay, ay; it goes all one way.

Neverout: Pray, miss, what's a clock?

Miss: Why, you must know, 'tis a thing like a bell, and you are a fool that can't tell.

Neverout [*to* Lady Answ]: Pray, madam, do you tell me? for I have let my watch run down.

Lady Answ: Why, 'tis half an hour past hanging time.

Col: Well, I'm like the butcher that was looking for his knife, and had it in his mouth: I have been searching my pockets for my snuff box, and, egad, here it is in my hand.

Miss: If it had been a bear, it would have bit you, Colonel: well I wish I had such a snuff box.

Neverout: You'll be long enough before you wish your skin full of eyelet holes.

Col: Wish in one hand –

Miss: Out upon you; Lord, what can the man mean?

Ld Sparkish: This tea is very hot.

Lady Answ: Why, it came from a hot place, my lord.

Colonel *spills his tea*

Lady Smart: That's as well done as if I had done myself.

Col: Madam, I find you live by ill neighbours, when you are forced to praise yourself.

Lady Smart: So they prayed me to tell you.

Neverout: Well, I won't drink a drop more; If I do, 'twill go down like chopped hay.

Miss: Pray, don't say no, till you are asked.

Neverout: Well, what you please, and the rest ill.

MISS: I have heard 'em say, that a pin a day is a groat a year.
Well, as I hope to be married, forgive me for swearing,
I vow 'tis a needle.

COL: Oh! the wonderful works of nature, that a black hen
should lay a white egg!

NEVEROUT: What! you have found a mare's nest, and laugh
at the eggs?[24]

MISS: Pray keep your breath to cool your porridge.

NEVEROUT: Miss, there was a very pleasant accident last
night at St James's Park.

MISS [*to* LADY SMART]: What was it your ladyship was going
to say just now?

NEVEROUT: Well, miss: tell a mare a tale –

MISS: I find you love to hear yourself talk.

NEVEROUT: Why, if you won't hear my tale, kiss my, etc.

MISS: Out upon you, for a filthy creature!

NEVEROUT: What, miss! must I tell you a story and find you
ears?

LD. SPARKISH [*to* LADY SMART]: Pray, madam, don't you
think Mrs Spendall very genteel?

LADY SMART: Why, my lord, I think she was cut out for a
gentlewoman, but she was spoiled in the making; she wears
her clothes as if they were thrown on her with a pitchfork;
and, for the fashion, I believe they were made in the reign
of Queen Bess.

NEVEROUT: Well, that's neither here nor there; for you know,
the more careless the more modish.

COL: Well, I'd hold a wager there will be a match between her
and Dick Dolt: and I believe I can see as far into a millstone
as another man.

MISS: Colonel, I must beg your pardon a thousand times; but they say, an old ape has an old eye.

NEVEROUT: Miss, what do you mean? you'll spoil the Colonel's marriage, if you call him old.

COL: Not so old, nor yet so cold – you know the rest, miss.

MISS: Manners is a fine thing, truly.

COL: 'Faith, miss, depend upon't, I'll give you as good as you bring: what! if you give a jest you must take a jest.

LADY SMART: Well, Mr Neverout, you'll ne'er have done till you break that knife, and then the man won't take it again.

MISS: Why, madam, fools will be meddling; I wish he may cut his fingers. I hope you can see your own blood without fainting.

NEVEROUT: Why, miss, you shine this morning like a shitten barn door: you'll never hold out at this rate; pray save a little wit for tomorrow.

MISS: Well, you have said your say; if people will be rude, I have done; my comfort is, 'twill be all one a thousand years hence.

NEVEROUT: Miss, you have shot your bolt: I find you must have the last word – Well, I'll go to the opera tonight – No, I can't, neither, for I have some business – and yet I think I must; for I promised to squire the Countess to her box.

MISS: The Countess of Puddledock, I suppose?

NEVEROUT: Peace, or war, miss?

LADY SMART: Well, Mr Neverout, you'll never be mad, you are of so many minds.

As MISS *rises, the chair falls behind her*

MISS: Well; I shan't be lady mayoress this year.

NEVEROUT: No, miss, 'tis worse than that; you won't be married this year.

MISS: Lord! you make me laugh, though I an't well.

NEVEROUT, *as* MISS *is standing,
pulls her suddenly on his lap*

NEVEROUT: Now, Colonel, come sit down on my lap; more sacks upon the mill.

MISS: Let me go; aren't you sorry for my heaviness?

NEVEROUT: No, miss; you are very light; but I don't say you are a light hussy. Pray take up the chair for your pains.

MISS: 'Tis but one body's labour, you may do it yourself; I wish you would be quiet, you have more tricks than a dancing bear.

NEVEROUT *rises to take up the chair,
and* MISS *sits in his*

NEVEROUT: You wouldn't be so soon in my grave, madam.

MISS: Lord! I have torn my petticoat with your odious romping; my rents are coming in; I'm afraid I shall fall into the ragman's hands.

NEVEROUT: I'll mend it, miss.

MISS: You mend it! go, teach your grannam to suck eggs.

NEVEROUT: Why, miss, you are so cross, I could find in my heart to hate you.

MISS: With all my heart; there will be no love lost between us.

NEVEROUT: But pray, my Lady Smart, does not miss look as if she could eat me without salt?

MISS: I'll make you one day sup sorrow for this.

NEVEROUT: Well, follow your own way, you'll live the longer.

MISS: See, madam, how well I have mended it.

LADY SMART: 'Tis indifferent, as Doll danced.

NEVEROUT: 'Twill last as many nights as days.

MISS: Well, I knew it should never have your good word.

LADY SMART: My lord, my Lady Answerall and I was walking in the park last night till near eleven; 'twas a very fine night.

NEVEROUT: Egad, so was I; and I'll tell you a comical accident; egad, I lost my understanding.

MISS: I'm glad you had any to lose.

LADY SMART: Well, but what do you mean?

NEVEROUT: Egad, I kicked my foot against a stone, and tore off the heel of my shoe, and was forced to limp to a cobbler in the Pall Mall to have it put on. He, he, he, he.

[*All laugh.*]

COL: O! 'twas a delicate night to run away with another man's wife.

NEVEROUT *sneezes*

MISS: God bless you! if you han't taken snuff.

NEVEROUT: Why, what if I have, miss?

MISS: Why then, the deuce take you!

NEVEROUT: Miss, I want that diamond ring of yours.

MISS: Why, then want's like to be your master.

NEVEROUT *looking at the ring*

NEVEROUT: Ay, marry, this is not only, but also: where did you get it?

MISS: Why, where 'twas to be had; where the devil got the friar.

NEVEROUT: Well; if I had such a fine diamond ring,
I wouldn't stay a day in England: but you know, far fetched

and dear bought is fit for ladies. I warrant, this cost your father twopence halfpenny.

COLONEL *stretching himself*

LADY SMART: Why, Colonel, you break the king's laws; you stretch without a halter.

LADY ANSW: Colonel, some ladies of your acquaintance have promised to breakfast with you, and I am to wait on them; what will you give us?

COL: Why, faith, madam, bachelor's fare; bread and cheese and kisses.

LADY ANSW: Poh! what have you bachelors to do with your money, but to treat the ladies? you have nothing to keep, but your own four quarters.

LADY SMART: My lord, has Captain Brag the honour to be related to your lordship?

LD SPARKISH: Very nearly, madam; he's my cousin-german quite removed.

LADY ANSW: Pray, is he not rich?

LD SPARKISH: Ay, a rich rogue, two shirts and a rag.

COL: Well, however, they say he has a great estate, but only the right owner keeps him out of it.

LADY SMART: What religion is he of?

LD SPARKISH: Why he is an Anythingarian.

LADY ANSW: I believe he has his religion to choose, my Lord.

NEVEROUT *scratches his head*

MISS: Fie, Mr Neverout, aren't you ashamed! I beg pardon for the expression, but I'm afraid your bosom friends are become your backbiters.

NEVEROUT: Well, miss, I saw a flea once in your pinner, and a louse is a man's companion, but a flea is a dog's companion: however, I wish you would scratch my neck with your pretty white hand.

MISS: And who would be fool then? I wouldn't touch a man's flesh for the universe. You have the wrong sow by the ear, I assure you; that's meat for your master.

NEVEROUT: Miss Notable, all quarrels laid aside, pray step hither for a moment.

MISS: I'll wash my hands and wait on you, sir; but pray come hither, and try to open this lock.

NEVEROUT: We'll try what we can do.

MISS: We! – what have you pigs in your belly?

NEVEROUT: Miss, I assure you I am very handy at all things.

MISS: Marry, hang them that can't give themselves a good word; I believe you may have an even hand to throw a louse in the fire.

COL: Well, I must be plain; here's a very bad smell.

MISS: Perhaps, Colonel, the fox is the finder.

NEVEROUT: No, Colonel; 'tis only your teeth against rain: but –

MISS: Colonel, I find you would make a very bad poor man's sow.

COLONEL *coughing*

COL: I have got a sad cold.

LADY ANSW: Ay; 'tis well if one can get anything these hard times.

MISS [*to* COL]: Choke, chicken, there's more a-hatching.

LADY SMART: Pray, Colonel, how did you get that cold?

LADY SPARKISH. Why, madam, I suppose the Colonel got it by lying abed barefoot.

LADY ANSW: Why, then, Colonel, you must take it for better for worse, as a man takes his wife.

COL: Well, ladies, I apprehend you without a constable.

MISS: Mr Neverout! Mr Neverout! come hither this moment.

LADY SMART [*imitating her*]: Mr Neverout! Mr Neverout! I wish he were tied to your girdle.

NEVEROUT: What's the matter? whose mare's dead now?

MISS: Take your labour for your pains, you may go back again, like a fool as you came.

NEVEROUT: Well, miss, if you deceive me a second time, 'tis my fault.

LADY SMART: Colonel, methinks your coat is too short.

COL: It will be long enough before I get another, madam.

MISS: Come, come; the coat's a good coat, and come of good friends.

NEVEROUT: Ladies, you are mistaken in the stuff; 'tis half silk.

COL: Tom Neverout, you are a fool, and that's your fault.

A great noise below

LADY SMART: Hey, what a clattering is here! one would think Hell was broke loose.

MISS: Indeed, madam, I must take my leave, for I a'n't well.

LADY SMART: What! you are sick of the mulligrubs with eating chopped hay?[25]

MISS: No, indeed, madam; I'm sick and hungry, more need of a cook than a doctor.

LADY ANSW: Poor miss! she's sick as a cushion, she wants nothing but stuffing.

COL: If you are sick, you shall have a caudle of calf's eggs.

NEVEROUT: I can't find my gloves.

MISS: I saw the dog running away with some dirty thing a while ago.

COL: Miss, you have got my handkerchief; pray let me have it.

LADY SMART: No; keep it, miss; for they say possession is eleven points of the law.

MISS: Madam, he shall ne'er have it again; 'tis in hucksters' hands.

LADY ANSW: What! I see 'tis raining again.

LADY SPARKISH. Why, then, madam, we must do as they do in Spain.

MISS: Pray, my lord, how is that?

LD SPARKISH: Why, madam, we must let it rain.

MISS whispers LADY SMART

NEVEROUT: There's no whispering, but there's lying.

MISS: Lord! Mr Neverout, you are as pert as a pear-monger this morning.

NEVEROUT: Indeed, miss, you are very handsome.

MISS: Poh! I know that already; tell me news.

Somebody knocks at the door
Footman comes in

FOOTMAN (*to* COL:). An' please your honour, there's a man below wants to speak to you.

COL: Ladies, your pardon for a minute.

LADY SMART: Miss, I sent yesterday to know how you did, but you were gone abroad early.

MISS: Why, indeed, madam, I was hunched up in a hackney coach with three country acquaintance, who called upon me to take the air as far as Highgate.

LADY SMART: And had you a pleasant airing?

MISS: No, madam; it rained all the time; I was jolted to death; and the road was so bad, that I screamed every moment, and called to the coachman, Pray, friend, don't spill us.

NEVEROUT: So, miss, you were afraid that pride would have a fall.

MISS: Mr Neverout, when I want a fool, I'll send for you.

LD SPARKISH: Miss, didn't your left ear burn last night?

MISS: Pray why, my lord?

LD SPARKISH: Because I was then in some company where you were extolled to the skies, I assure you.

MISS: My lord, that was more their goodness than my desert.

LD SPARKISH: They said, that you were a complete beauty.

MISS: My lord, I am as God made me.

LADY SMART: The girl's well enough, if she had but another nose.

MISS: O! madam, I know I shall always have your good word; you love to help a lame dog over the stile.

One knocks

LADY SMART: Who's there? you're on the wrong side of the door; come in, if you be fat.

COLONEL *comes in again*

LD SPARKISH: Why, Colonel, you are a man of great business.

COL: Ay, ay, my lord, I'm like my lord mayor's fool, full of business and nothing to do.

LADY SMART: My lord, don't you think the Colonel's mightily fallen away of late?

LD SPARKISH: Ay, fallen from a horseload to a cartload.

COL: Why, my lord, egad, I am like a rabbit, fat and lean in four-and-twenty hours.

LADY SMART: I assure you, the Colonel walks as straight as a pin.

MISS: Yes; he's a handsome-bodied man in the face.

NEVEROUT: A handsome foot and leg; god-a-mercy shoe and stocking!

COL: What! three upon one! that's foul play: this would make a parson swear.

NEVEROUT: Why, miss, what's the matter? you look as if you had neither won or lost.

COL: Why you must know, miss lives upon love.

MISS: Yes, upon love and lumps of the cupboard.

LADY ANSW: Ay; they say love and pease porridge are two dangerous things; one breaks the heart, and the other the belly.

MISS [*imitating* LADY ANSWERALL's *tone*]: Very pretty! one breaks the heart, and the other the belly.

LADY ANSW: Have a care; they say, mocking is catching.

MISS: I never heard that.

NEVEROUT: Why, then, miss, you have a wrinkle – more than ever you had before.

MISS: Well; live and learn.

NEVEROUT: Ay; and be hanged and forget all.

MISS: Well, Mr Neverout, take it as you please; but, I swear, you are a saucy Jack, to use such expressions.

NEVEROUT: Why then, miss, if you go to that, I must tell you there's ne'er a Jack but there's a Gill.

MISS: Oh! Mr Neverout, everybody knows that you are the

pink of courtesy.

NEVEROUT: And, miss, all the world allows that you are the flower of civility.

LADY SMART: Miss, I hear there was a great deal of company where you visited last night: pray, who were they?

MISS: Why there was old Lady Forward, Miss To-and-again, Sir John Ogle, my Lady Clapper and I, quoth the dog.

COL: Was your visit long, miss?

MISS: Why, truly, they all went to the opera; and so poor Pilgarlick came home alone.

NEVEROUT: Alackaday, poor miss! Methinks it grieves me to pity you.

MISS: What! You think, you said a fine thing now; well, if I had a dog with no more wit, I would hang him.

LADY SMART: Miss, if it is manners, may I ask which is oldest, you or Lady Scuttle?

MISS: Why, my lord, when I die for age she may quake for fear.

LADY SMART: She's a very great gadder abroad.

LADY ANSW: Lord! she made me follow her last week through all the shops like a Tantiny pig.[26]

LADY SMART: I remember, you told me, you had been with her from Dan to Beersheba.

COLONEL *spits*

COL: Lord! I shall die; I cannot spit from me.

MISS: O! Mr Neverout, my little countess has just littered; speak me fair, and I'll set you down for a puppy.

NEVEROUT: Why, miss, if I speak you fair, perhaps I mayn't tell truth.

LD SPARKISH: Ay, but Tom, smoke that, she calls you puppy by craft.

NEVEROUT: Well, miss, you ride the fore horse today.

MISS: Ay, many a one says well, that thinks ill.

NEVEROUT: Fie, miss; you said that once before; and you know too much of one thing is good for nothing.

MISS: Why, sure we can't say a good thing too often.

LD SPARKISH: Well, so much for that, and butter for fish; let us call another cause. Pray, madam, does your ladyship know Mrs Nice?

LADY SMART: Perfectly well, my lord; she's nice by name, and nice by nature.

LD SPARKISH: Is it possible she could take that booby Tom Blunder for love?

MISS: She had good skill in horseflesh, that would choose a goose to ride on.

LADY ANSW: Why, my lord, 'twas her fate; they say, marriage and hanging go by destiny.

COL: I believe she'll never be burnt for a witch.

LD SPARKISH: They say, marriages are made in Heaven; but I doubt when she was married, she had no friend there.

NEVEROUT: Well, she's got out of God's blessing into the warm sun.

COL: The fellow's well enough if he had any guts in his brains.

LADY SMART: They say, thereby hangs a tale.

LD SPARKISH: Why, he's a mere hobbledehoy, neither a man nor a boy.

MISS: Well, if I were to choose a husband, I would never be married to a little man.

NEVEROUT: Pray, why so, miss? for they say of all evils we ought to choose the least.

MISS: Because folks would say, when they saw us together, there goes the woman and her husband.

COL [*to* LADY SMART]: Will your ladyship be on the Mall tomorrow night?

LADY SMART: No, that won't be proper; you know tomorrow's Sunday.

LD SPARKISH: What then, madam! they say, the better day, the better deed.

LADY ANSW: Pray, Mr Neverout, how do you like Lady Fruzz?

NEVEROUT: Pox on her! she's as old as Poles.

MISS: So will you be, if you ben't hanged when you're young.

NEVEROUT: Come, miss, let us be friends: will you go to the park this evening?

MISS: With all my heart, and a piece of my liver; but not with you.

LADY SMART: I'll tell you one thing, and that's not two; I'm afraid I shall get a fit of the headache today.

COL: O! madam, don't be afraid; it comes with a fright.

MISS [*to* LADY ANSWERALL]: Madam, one of your ladyship's lappets is longer than t'other.

LADY ANSW: Well, no matter; they that ride on a trotting horse will ne'er perceive it.

NEVEROUT: Indeed, miss, your lappets hang worse.

MISS: Well, I love a liar in my heart, and you fit me to a hair.

MISS *rises up*

NEVEROUT: Deuce take you, miss; you trod on my foot: I hope you don't intend to come to my bedside.

MISS: In troth, you are afraid of your friends, and none of them near you.

LD SPARKISH: Well said, girl! [*giving her a chuck*] take that: they say a chuck under the chin is worth two kisses.

LADY ANSW: But, Mr Neverout, I wonder why such a handsome, straight, young gentleman as you don't get some rich widow.

LD SPARKISH: Straight! ay, straight as my leg, as that's crooked at knee.

NEVEROUT: 'Faith, madam, if it rained rich widows, none of them would fall upon me. Egad, I was born under a threepenny planet, never to be worth a groat.

LADY ANSW: No, Mr Neverout: I believe you were born with a caul on your head; you are such a favourite among the ladies: but what think you of widow Prim? she's immensely rich.

NEVEROUT: Hang her! they say her father was a baker.

LADY SMART: Ay; but it is not, what is she, but what has she, nowadays.

COL: Tom, 'faith, put on a bold face for once, And have at the widow. I'll speak a good word for you to her.

LADY ANSW: Ay; I warrant you'll speak one word for him, and two for yourself.

MISS: Well; I had that at my tongue's end.

LADY ANSW: Why, miss, they say, good wits jump.

NEVEROUT: 'Faith, Madam, I had rather marry a woman I loved, in her smock, than widow Prim, if she had her weight in gold.

LADY SMART: Come, come, Mr Neverout, marriage is honourable, but housekeeping is a shrew.

LADY ANSW: Consider, Mr Neverout, four bare legs in a bed, and you are a younger brother.

COL: Well, madam; the younger brother is the better gentleman; however, Tom, I would advise you to look before you leap.

LD SPARKISH: The colonel says true; besides, you can't expect to wive and thrive in the same year.

MISS [*shuddering*]: Lord! there's somebody walking over my grave.

COL: Pray, Lady Answerall, where was you last Wednesday, when I did myself the honour to wait on you? I think your ladyship is one of the tribe of Gad.

LADY ANSW: Why, Colonel, I was at church.

COL: Nay, then will I be hanged, and my horse too.

NEVEROUT: I believe her ladyship was at a church with a chimney in it.

MISS: Lord, my petticoat! how it hangs by jommetry!

NEVEROUT: Perhaps the fault may be in your shape.

MISS [*looking gravely*]: Come, Mr Neverout, there's no jest like the true jest; but I suppose you think my back's broad enough to bear everything.

NEVEROUT: Madam, I humbly beg your pardon.

MISS: Well, sir, your pardon's granted.

NEVEROUT: Well, all things have an end, and a pudding has two, up-up-on me-my-my word [*stutters*].

MISS: What! Mr Neverout, can't you speak without a spoon?

LD SPARKISH [*to* LADY SMART]: Has your ladyship seen the duchess since your falling out?

LADY SMART: Never, my lord, but once at a visit; And she looked at me as the devil looked over Lincoln.

NEVEROUT: Pray, miss, take a pinch of my snuff.

MISS: What! you break my head, and give me a plaster; well, with all my heart; once, and not use it.

NEVEROUT: Well, miss, if you wanted me and your victuals, you'd want your two best friends.

COL [*to* NEVEROUT]: Tom, miss and you must kiss and be friends.

NEVEROUT *salutes* MISS

69

MISS: Anything for a quiet life: my nose itched, and I knew I should drink wine, or kiss a fool.

COL: Well, Tom, if that ben't fair, hang fair.

NEVEROUT: I never said a rude thing to a lady in my life.

MISS: Here's a pin for that lie; I'm sure liars had need have good memories. Pray, Colonel, was not he very uncivil to me but just now?

LADY ANSW: Mr Neverout, if miss will be angry for nothing, take my counsel, and bid her turn the buckle of her girdle behind her.

NEVEROUT: Come, Lady Answerall, I know better things; miss and I are good friends; don't put tricks upon travellers.

COL: Tom, not a word of the pudding, I beg you.

LADY SMART: Ah, Colonel! you'll never be good nor then neither.

LD SPARKISH: Which of the goods d'ye mean? good for something, or good for nothing?

MISS: I have a blister on my tongue; yet I don't remember I told a lie.

LADY ANSW: I thought you did just now.

LD SPARKISH: Pray, madam, what did thought do?

LADY ANSW: Well, for my life, I cannot conceive what your lordship means.

LD SPARKISH: Indeed, madam, I meant no harm.

LADY SMART: No, to be sure, my lord! you are as innocent as a devil of two years old.

NEVEROUT: Madam, they say, ill-doers are ill deemers; but I don't apply it to your ladyship.

MISS *mending a hole in her lace*

MISS: Well, you see, I'm mending; I hope I shall be good in time; look, Lady Answerall, is it not well mended?

LADY ANSW: Ay, this is something like a tansy.

NEVEROUT: 'Faith, miss, you have mended, as a tinker mends a kettle; stop one hole, and make two.

LADY SMART: Pray, Colonel, are you not very much tann'd?

COL: Yes, madam; but a cup of Christmas ale will soon wash it off.

LD SPARKISH: Lady Smart, does not your ladyship think Mrs Fade is mightily altered since her marriage?

LADY ANSW: Why, my lord, she was handsome in her time; but she cannot eat her cake and have her cake; I hear she's grown a mere otomy.[27]

LADY SMART: Poor creature! the black ox has set his foot upon her already.

MISS: Ay; she has quite lost the blue on the plum.

LADY SMART: And yet, they say, her husband is very fond of her still.

LADY ANSW: O, madam, if she would eat gold, he would give it her.

NEVEROUT [*to* LADY SMART]: Madam, have you heard that Lady Queasy was lately at the playhouse incog.?

LADY SMART: What! Lady Queasy of all women in the world! do you say it upon rep.?

NEVEROUT: Poz, I saw her with my own eyes; she sat among the mob in the gallery; her own ugly phiz; and she saw me look at her.

COL: Her ladyship was plaguily bamb'd; I warrant it put her into the hips.

NEVEROUT: I smoked her huge nose, and, egad, she put me in mind of the woodcock, that strives to hide his long bill, and then thinks nobody sees him.

Col: Tom, I advise you, hold your tongue; for you'll never say so good a thing again.

Lady Smart: Miss, what are you looking for?

Miss: O, madam, I have lost the finest needle –

Lady Answ: Why, seek till you find it, and then you won't lose your labour.

Neverout: The loop of my hat is broke; how shall I mend it? [*He fastens it with a pin.*] Well, hang him, say I, that has no shift.

Miss: Ay, and hang him that has one too many.

Neverout: O, miss, I have heard a sad story of you.

Miss: I defy you, Mr Neverout; nobody can say, black's my eye.

Neverout: I believe you wish they could.

Miss: Well; but who was your author? Come, tell truth, and shame the devil.

Neverout: Come then, miss; guess who it was that told me; come, put on your considering cap.

Miss: Well, who was it?

Neverout: Why, one that lives within a mile of an oak.

Miss: Well, go hang yourself in your own garters, for I'm sure the gallows groans for you.

Neverout: Pretty miss! I was but in jest.

Miss: Well, but don't let that stick in your gizzard.

Col: My lord, does your Lordship know Mrs Talkall?

Ld Sparkish: Only by sight; but I hear she has a great deal of wit; and, egad, as the saying is, mettle to the back.

Lady Smart: So I hear.

Col: Why Dick Lubber said to her t'other day: 'Madam, you can't cry Bo to a goose.' 'Yes, but I can,' said she, and egad, cried Bo full in his face. We all thought we should break our hearts with laughing.

LD SPARKISH: That was cutting with a vengeance; and prithee how did the fool look?

COL: Look! egad, he looked for all the world like an owl in an ivy bush.

A child comes in screaming

MISS: Well, if that child was mine, I'd whip it till the blood came; peace, you little vixen! If I were near you, I would not be far from you.

LADY SMART: Ay, ay! bachelors' wives and maids' children are finely tutored.

LADY ANSW: Come to me, master, and I'll give you a sugarplum. Why, miss, you forget that ever you was a child yourself [*she gives the child a lump of sugar*]: I have heard 'em say, boys will long.

COL: My lord, I suppose you know that Mr Buzzard has married again.

LADY SMART: This is his fourth wife; then he has been shod round.

COL: Why, you must know, she had a month's mind to Dick Frontless, and thought to run away with him, but her parents forced her to take the old fellow for a good settlement.

LD SPARKISH: So the man got his mare again.

LADY SMART: I'm told he said a very good thing to Dick. Said he: 'You think us old fellows are fools; but we old fellows know young fellows are fools.'

COL: I know nothing of that; but I know he's devilish old, and she's very young.

LADY ANSW: Why, they call that a match of the world's making.

MISS: What if he had been young and she old?

NEVEROUT: Why, miss, that would have been a match of the devil's making; but when both are young that's a match of God's making.

MISS *searching her pocket for a thimble,*
brings out a nutmeg

NEVEROUT: Oh, miss, have a care, for if you carry a nutmeg in your pocket, you'll certainly be married to an old man.

MISS: Well, if I ever be married it shall be to an old man; they always make the best husbands, and it is better to be an old man's darling than a young man's warling.[28]

NEVEROUT: 'Faith, miss, if you speak as you think, I'll give you my mother for a maid.

LADY SMART *rings the bell*
Footman comes in

LADY SMART: Harkee, you fellow, run to my Lady Match, and desire she will remember to be here at six to play at quadrille; d'ye hear, if you fall by the way don't stay to get up again.

FOOTMAN: Madam, I don't know the house.

LADY SMART: That's not for want of ignorance; follow your nose; go, enquire among the servants.

Footman goes out and leaves the door open

LADY SMART: Here, come back, you fellow; why did you leave the door open? Remember that a good servant must always come when he's call'd, do what he's bid, and shut the door after him.

The footman goes out again, and falls downstairs

LADY ANSW: Neck or nothing; come down, or I'll fetch you down; well, but I hope the poor fellow has not saved the hangman a labour.

NEVEROUT: Pray, madam, smoke miss yonder, biting her lips and playing with her fan.

MISS: Who's that takes my name in vain?

She runs up to them, and falls down

LADY SMART: What, more falling! do you intend the frolic should go round?

LADY ANSW: Why, miss, I wish you may not have broke her ladyship's floor.

NEVEROUT: Miss, come to me, and I'll take you up.

LADY SPARKISH. Well, but without a jest, I hope, miss, you are not hurt.

COL: Nay, she must be hurt for certain, for you see her head is all of a lump.

MISS: Well, remember this, Colonel, when I have money and you have none.

LADY SMART: But Colonel, when do you design to get a house, and a wife, and a fire to put her in?

MISS: Lord! who would be married to a soldier and carry his knapsack?

NEVEROUT: O, madam, Mars and Venus, you know.

COL: Egad, madam, I'd marry tomorrow, if I thought I could bury my wife just when the honeymoon is over; but they say a woman has as many lives as a cat.

LADY ANSW: I find, the colonel thinks a dead wife under the table is the best goods in a man's house.

LADY SMART: Oh, but Colonel, if you had a good wife, it would break your heart to part with her.

COL: Yes, madam; for they say, he that has lost his wife and sixpence has lost a tester.[29]

LADY SMART: But, Colonel, they say, that every married man should believe there's but one good wife in the world, and that's his own.

COL: For all that, I doubt, a good wife must be bespoke; for there's none ready made.

MISS: I suppose, the gentleman's a woman-hater; but, sir, I think you ought to remember that you had a mother, and pray, if it had not been for a woman, where would you have been, Colonel?

COL: Nay, miss, you cried whore first, when you talked of the knapsack.

LADY ANSW: But I hope you won't blame the whole sex, because some are bad.

NEVEROUT: And they say, he that hates woman sucked a sow.

COL: Oh, madam, there's no general rule without an exception.

LADY SMART: Then, why don't you marry, and settle?

COL: Egad, madam, there's nothing will settle me but a bullet.

LD SPARKISH: Well, Colonel, there's one comfort, that you need not fear a cannon-bullet.

COL: Why so, my lord?

LD SPARKISH: Because they say he was cursed in his mother's belly that was killed by a cannon-bullet.

MISS: I suppose the colonel was crossed in his first love, which makes him so severe on all the sex.

LADY ANSW: Yes; and I'll hold a hundred to one that the colonel has been over head and ears in love with some lady that has made his heart ache.

COL: Oh, madam, we soldiers are admirers of all the fair sex.

MISS: I wish I could see the colonel in love till he was ready to die.

LADY SMART: Ay, but I doubt, few people die for love in these days.

NEVEROUT: Well, I confess, I differ from the colonel, for I hope to have a rich and a handsome wife yet before I die.

COL: Ay, Tom; live, horse, and thou shalt have grass.

MISS: Well, Colonel; but whatever you say against women, they are better creatures than men, for men were made of clay, but woman was made of man.

COL: Miss, you may say what you please; but 'faith you'll never lead apes in Hell.

NEVEROUT: No, no; I'll be sworn miss has not an inch of nun's flesh about her.

MISS: I understumble you, gentlemen.

NEVEROUT: Madam, your humblecumdumble.[30]

LD SPARKISH: Pray, miss, when did you see your old acquaintance, Mrs Cloudy? you and she are two I hear.

MISS: See her; marry, I don't care whether I ever see her again! God bless my eyesight.

LADY ANSW: Lord! why she and you were as great as two inkle weavers.[31] I've seen her hug you as the devil hugged the witch.

MISS: That's true; but I'm told for certain, she's no better than she should be.

LADY SMART: Well, God mend us all; but you must allow, the world is very censorious; I never heard that she was a naughty pack.

COL [to NEVEROUT]: Come, Sir Thomas, when the King pleases, when do you intend to march?

LD SPARKISH: Have a patience. Tom, is your friend Ned Rattle married?

NEVEROUT: Yes, 'faith, my lord; he has tied a knot with his tongue, that he can never untie with his teeth.

LADY SMART: Ah! marry in haste and repent at leisure.

LADY ANSW: Has he got a good fortune with his lady? for they say, something has some savour, but nothing has no flavour.

NEVEROUT: 'Faith, madam, all he gets by her he may put into his eye and see never the worse.

MISS: Then, I believe, he heartily wishes her in Abraham's bosom.

COL: Pray, my lord, how does Charles Limber and his fine wife agree?

LD SPARKISH: Why they say he's the greatest cuckold in town.

NEVEROUT: Oh, but my lord, you should always except my Lord Mayor.

MISS: Mr Neverout!

NEVEROUT: Hay, madam, did you call me?

MISS: Hay! Why hay is for horses.

NEVEROUT: Why, miss, then you may kiss –

COL: Pray, my lord, what's o'clock by your oracle?

LD SPARKISH: 'Faith, I can't tell, I think my watch runs upon wheels.

NEVEROUT: Miss, pray be so kind to call a servant to bring me a glass of small beer; I know you are at home here.

MISS: Every fool can do as they're bid; make a page of your own age, and do it yourself.

NEVEROUT: Choose, proud fool; I did but ask you.

MISS *puts her hand upon her knee*

NEVEROUT: What, miss, are you thinking of your sweetheart? Is your garter slipping down?

MISS: Pray, Mr Neverout, keep your breath to cool your porridge; you measure my corn by your bushel.

NEVEROUT: Indeed, miss, you lie –

MISS: Did you ever hear anything so rude?

NEVEROUT: I mean you lie – under a mistake.

MISS: If a thousand lies could choke you, you would have been choked many a day ago.

MISS tries to snatch MR NEVEROUT'S *snuff box*

NEVEROUT: Madam, you missed that, as you missed your mother's blessing.

She tries again and misses

NEVEROUT: Snap short makes you look so lean, miss.

MISS: Poh! you are so robustious, you had like to put out my eye; I assure you, if you blind me, you must lead me.

LADY SMART: Dear miss, be quiet, and bring me a pincushion out of that closet.

MISS opens the closet-door and squalls

LADY SMART: Lord bless the girl! what's the matter now?

MISS: I vow, madam, I saw something in black: I thought it was a spirit.

COL: Why, miss, did you ever see a spirit?

MISS: No, sir; I thank God I never saw anything worse than myself.

NEVEROUT: Well, I did a very foolish thing yesterday, and was a great puppy[32] for my pains.

MISS: Very likely; for they say, many a true word's spoke in jest.

Footman returns

LADY SMART: Well, did you deliver your message? You are fit to be sent for sorrow, you stay so long by the way.

FOOTMAN: Madam, my lady was not at home, so I did not leave the message.

LADY SMART: This it is to send a fool of an errand.

LD SPARKISH [*looking at his watch*]: 'Tis past twelve o'clock.

LADY SMART: Well, what is that among all us?

LD SPARKISH: Madam, I must take my leave: come, gentlemen, are you for a march?

LADY SMART: Well, but your Lordship and the colonel will dine with us today; and, Mr Neverout, I hope we shall have your good company: there will be no soul else, beside my own lord and these ladies; for everybody knows I hate a crowd; I would rather want victuals than elbow room; we dine punctually at three.

LD SPARKISH: Madam, we'll be sure to attend your ladyship.

COL: Madam, my stomach serves me instead of a clock.

Another footman comes back

LADY SMART: O! you are the t'other fellow I sent; well, have you been with my Lady Club? You are good to send of a dead man's errand.

FOOTMAN: Madam, my Lady Club begs your ladyship's pardon; but she is engaged tonight.

MISS: Well, Mr Neverout, here's the back of my hand to you.

NEVEROUT: Miss, I find you will have the last word. Ladies, I am more yours than my own.

DIALOGUE II

*Lord Smart and the former company at
three o' clock coming to dine.
After salutations*

LORD SMART: I'm sorry I was not at home this morning
when you all did us the honour to call here; but I went to
the levee today.

LD SPARKISH: O! my lord; I'm sure the loss was ours.

LADY SMART: Gentlemen and ladies, you are come to a sad
dirty house; I am sorry for it, but we have had our hands
in mortar.

LD SPARKISH: O! madam, your ladyship is pleased to say so;
but I never saw anything so clean and so fine; I profess, it is
a perfect paradise.

LADY SMART: My lord, your lordship is always very obliging.

LD SPARKISH: Pray, madam, whose picture is that?

LADY SMART: Why, my lord, it was drawn for me.

LD SPARKISH: I'll swear the painter did not flatter your
ladyship.

COL: My lord, the day is finely cleared up.

LD SMART: Ay, Colonel; 'tis a pity that fair weather should
ever do any harm. [*to* NEVEROUT] Why, Tom, you are high
in the mode.

NEVEROUT: My lord, it is better to be out of the world than
out of the fashion.

LD SMART: But, Tom, I hear you and miss are always
quarrelling: I fear it is your fault; for I can assure you she is
very good-humoured.

NEVEROUT: Ay, my lord; so is the devil when he's pleased.

LD SMART: Miss, what do you think of my friend Tom?

Miss: My lord, I think he's not the wisest man in the world; and truly he's sometimes very rude.

Ld Sparkish: That may be true; but yet he that hangs Tom for a fool, may find a knave in halter.

Miss: Well, however, I wish he were hanged, if it were only to try.

Neverout: Well, miss, if I must be hanged, I won't go far to choose my gallows; it shall be about your fair neck.

Miss: I'll see your nose cheese first, and the dogs eating it. But, my lord, Mr Neverout's wit begins to run low: for I vow he said this before; pray, Colonel, give him a pinch, and I'll do as much for you.

Ld Sparkish: My Lady Smart, your ladyship has a very fine scarf.

Lady Smart: Yes, my lord, it will make a flaming figure in a country church.

Footman comes in

Footman: Madam, dinner's upon the table.

Col: 'Faith, I am glad of it; my belly began to cry cupboard.

Neverout: I wish I may never hear worse news.

Miss: What! Mr Neverout, you are in great haste; I believe your belly thinks your throat is cut.

Neverout: No, 'faith, miss; three meals a day, and a good supper at night, will serve my turn.

Miss: To say the truth, I'm hungry.

Neverout: And I'm angry; so let us both go fight.

*They go in to dinner, and,
after the usual compliments, take their seats*

LADY SMART: Ladies and gentlemen, will you eat any oysters before dinner?

COL: With all my heart [*takes an oyster*]. He was a bold man that first eat an oyster.

LADY SMART: They say oysters are a cruel meat, because we eat them alive; then they are an uncharitable meat, for we leave nothing to the poor; and they are an ungodly meat, because we never say grace.

NEVEROUT: 'Faith, that's as well said as if I had said it myself.

LADY SMART: Well, we are well set if we be but as well served. Come, Colonel, handle your arms. Shall I help you to some beef?

COL: If your ladyship please: and, pray, don't cut like a mother-in-law, but send me a large slice, for I love to lay a good foundation. I vow, 'tis a noble sirloin.

NEVEROUT: Ay, here's cut and come again.

MISS: But, pray, why is it called a sirloin?

LADY SMART: Why, you must know that our King James the First, who loved good eating, being invited to dinner by one of his nobles, and seeing a large loin of beef at his table, he drew out his sword, and in a frolic knighted it. Few people know the secret of this.

LADY SPARKISH. Beef is man's meat, my lord.

LD SMART: But, my lord, I say beef is the king of meat.

MISS: Pray, what have I done that I must not have a plate?

LADY SMART [*to* LADY ANSW]: What will your ladyship please to eat?

LADY ANSW: Pray, madam, help yourself.

COL: They say eating and scratching wants but a beginning: if you'll give me leave, I'll help myself to a slice of this shoulder of veal.

LADY SMART: Colonel, you can't do a kinder thing: well, you are all heartily welcome, as I may say.

COL: They say there are thirty and two good bits in a shoulder of veal.

LADY SMART: Ay, Colonel, thirty bad bits and two good ones; you see I understand you; but I hope you have got one of the two good ones.

NEVEROUT: Colonel, I'll be of your mess.

COL: Then pray, Tom, carve for yourself; they say, two hands in a dish, and one in a purse. Hah! said I well, Tom?

NEVEROUT: Colonel, you spoke like an oracle.

MISS [*to* LADY ANSW]: Madam, will your ladyship help me to some fish?

LD SMART [*to* NEVEROUT]: Tom, they say fish should swim thrice.

NEVEROUT: How is that, my lord?

LD SMART: Why, Tom, first it should swim in the sea (do you mind me?), then it should swim in butter, and at last, sirrah, it should swim in good claret. I think I have made it out.

FOOTMAN [*to* LD SMART]: My lord, Sir John Linger is coming up.

LD SMART: God so! I invited him to dine with me today, and forgot it: well, desire him to walk in.

SIR JOHN LINGER *comes in*

SIR JOHN: What! you are at it! why, then, I'll be gone.

LADY SMART: Sir John, I beg you will sit down; come, the more the merrier.

SIR JOHN: Ay; but the fewer the better cheer.

LADY SMART: Well, I am the worst in the world at making

apologies; it was my lord's fault: I doubt you must kiss the hare's foot.

SIR JOHN: I see you are fast by the teeth.

COL: 'Faith, Sir John, we are killing that that would kill us.

LD SPARKISH: You see, Sir John, we are upon a business of life and death. Come, will you do as we do? You are come in pudding-time.

SIR JOHN: Ay; this would be doing if I were dead. What! you keep court hours I see: I'll be going, and get a bit of meat at my inn.

LADY SMART: Why, we won't eat you, Sir John.

SIR JOHN: It is my own fault; but I was kept by a fellow who bought some Derbyshire oxen of me.

NEVEROUT: You see, Sir John, we stayed for you as one horse does for another.

LADY SMART: My lord, will you help Sir John to some beef? Lady Answerall, pray eat: you see your dinner. I am sure, if we had known we should have such good company, we should have been better provided; but you must take the will for the deed. I'm afraid you are invited to your loss.

COL: And pray, Sir John, how do you like the town? You have been absent a long time.

SIR JOHN: Why, I find little London stands just here it did when I left it last.

NEVEROUT: What do you think of Hanover Square? Why, Sir John, London is gone out of town since you saw it.

LADY SMART: Sir John, I can only say, you are heartily welcome; and I wish I had something better for you.

COL: Here's no salt; cuckolds will run away with the meat.

LD SMART: Pray edge a little, to make more room for Sir John. Sir John, fall to; you know, half an hour is soon lost at dinner.

SIR JOHN: I protest, I can't eat a bit, for I took share of a beef-steak and two mugs of ale with my chapman, besides a tankard of March beer, as soon as I got out of my bed.

LADY ANSW: Not fresh and fasting, I hope?

SIR JOHN: Yes, 'faith, madam; I always wash my kettle before I put the meat in it.

LADY SMART: Poh! Sir John, you have seen nine houses since you eat last. Come, you have kept a corner in your stomach for a piece of venison pasty.

SIR JOHN: Well, I'll try what I can do when it comes up.

LADY ANSW: Come, Sir John, you may go further and fare worse.

MISS [*to* NEVEROUT]: Pray, Mr Neverout, will you please to send me a piece of tongue?

NEVEROUT: By no means, madam; one tongue's enough for a woman.

COL: Miss, here's a tongue that never told a lie.

MISS: That was because it could not speak. Why, Colonel, I never told a lie in my life.

NEVEROUT: I appeal to all the company, whether that be not the greatest lie that ever was told?

COL [*to* NEVEROUT]: Prithee, Tom, send me the two legs and rump and liver of that pigeon; for, you must know, I love what nobody else loves.

NEVEROUT: But what if any of the ladies should long? Well, here take it, and the devil do you good with it.

LADY ANSW: Well; this eating and drinking takes away a body's stomach.

NEVEROUT: I am sure I have lost mine.

MISS: What! the bottom of it, I suppose?

NEVEROUT: No, really, miss, I have quite lost it.

MISS: I should be very sorry a poor body had found it.

LADY SMART: But, Sir John, we hear you are married since we saw you last. What! you have stolen a wedding, it seems?

SIR JOHN: Well; one can't do a foolish thing once in one's life, but one must hear of it a hundred times.

COL: And pray, Sir John, how does your lady unknown?

SIR JOHN: My wife's well, Colonel, and at your service in a civil way. Ha, ha!

[*He laughs.*]

MISS: Pray, Sir John, is your lady tall or short?

SIR JOHN: Why, miss, I thank God, she is a little evil.

LD SPARKISH: Come, give me a glass of claret.

Footman fills him a bumper

LD SPARKISH: Why do you fill so much?

NEVEROUT: My lord, he fills as he loves you.

LADY SMART: Miss, shall I send you some cucumber?

MISS: Madam, I dare not touch it: for they say, cucumbers are cold in the third degree.

LADY SMART: Mr Neverout, do you love pudding?

NEVEROUT: Madam, I'm like all fools, I love everything that is good; but the proof of the pudding is in the eating.

COL: Sir John, I hear you are a great walker when you are at home.

SIR JOHN: No, 'faith, Colonel; I always love to walk with a horse in my hand: but I have had devilish bad luck in horseflesh of late.

LD SMART: Why, then, Sir John, you must kiss a parson's wife.

LADY SMART: They say, Sir John, that your lady has a great deal of wit.

SIR JOHN: Madam, she can make a pudding; and has just wit enough to know her husband's breeches from another man's.

LD SMART: My Lord Sparkish, I have some excellent cider: will you please to taste it?

LD SPARKISH: My lord, I should like it well enough, if it were not treacherous.

LD SMART: Pray, my lord, how is it treacherous?

LD SPARKISH: Because it smiles in my face, and cuts my throat.

[*Here a loud laugh.*]

MISS: Odd so! madam; your knives are very sharp, for I have cut my finger.

LADY SMART: I am sorry for it: pray, which finger? (God bless the mark!)

MISS: Why, this finger: no, 'tis this: I vow I can't find which it is.

NEVEROUT: Ay; the fox had a wound and he could not tell where, etc. Bring some water to throw in her face.

MISS: Pray, Mr Neverout, did you ever draw a sword in anger? I warrant, you would faint at the sight of your own blood.

LADY SMART: Mr Neverout, shall I send you some veal?

NEVEROUT: No, madam; I don't love it.

MISS: Then pray for them that do. I desire your ladyship will send me a bit.

LD SMART: Tom, my service to you.

NEVEROUT: My lord, this moment I did myself the honour to drink to your lordship.

LD SMART: Why, then, that's Hertfordshire kindness.

NEVEROUT: 'Faith, my lord, I pledged myself; for I drank twice together without thinking.

LD SPARKISH: Why, then, Colonel, my humble service to you.

NEVEROUT: Pray, my lord, don't make a bridge of my nose.

LD SPARKISH: Well, a glass of this wine is as comfortable as matrimony to an old woman.

COL: Sir John, I design one of these days to come and beat up your quarters in Derbyshire.

SIR JOHN: 'Faith, Colonel, come and welcome: and stay away, and heartily welcome: but you were born within the sound of Bow bell, and don't care to stir so far from London.

MISS: Pray, Colonel, send me some fritters.

COLONEL *takes them out with his hand*

COL: Here, miss; they say fingers were made before forks, and hands before knives.

LADY SMART: Methinks this pudding is too much boiled.

LADY ANSW: O! madam, they say a pudding is poison when it is too much boiled.

NEVEROUT: Miss, shall I help you to a pigeon? here's a pigeon so finely roasted it cries, Come eat me.

MISS: No, sir; I thank you.

NEVEROUT: Why, then you may choose.

MISS: I have chosen already.

NEVEROUT: Well, you may be worse offered before you are twice married.

The COLONEL *fills a large plate of soup*

LD SMART: Why, Colonel, you don't mean to eat all that soup?

COL: O, my lord, this is my sick dish; when I'm well I'll have a bigger.

MISS [*to* COL]: Sup, Simon; very good broth.

NEVEROUT: This seems to be a good pullet.

MISS: I warrant, Mr Neverout knows what's good for himself.

LD SPARKISH: Tom, I shan't take your word for it; help me to a wing.

NEVEROUT *tries to cut off a wing*

NEVEROUT: Egad, I can't hit the joint.

LD SPARKISH: Why, then, think of a cuckold.

NEVEROUT: O, now I have nicked it.

[*Gives it to* LD SPARKISH]

LD SPARKISH: Why, a man may eat this, though his wife lay a dying.

COL: Pray, friend, give me a glass of small beer, if it be good.

LD SMART: Why, Colonel, they say there is no such thing as good small beer, good brown bread, or a good old woman.

LADY SMART [*to* LADY ANSW]: Madam, I beg your ladyship's pardon; I did not see you when I was cutting that bit.

LADY ANSW: O! madam; after you is good manners.

LADY SMART: Lord! here's a hair in the sauce.

LADY SPARKISH. Then set the hounds after it.

NEVEROUT: Pray, Colonel, help me however to some of that same sauce.

COL: Come, I think you are more sauce than pig.

LD SMART: Sir John, cheer up; my service to you: well, what do you think of the world to come?

SIR JOHN: Truly, my lord, I think of it as little as I can.

LADY SMART [*putting a skewer on a plate*]: Here, take this skewer, and carry it down to the cook, to dress it for her own dinner.

Neverout: I beg your ladyship's pardon; but this small beer is dead.

Lady Smart: Why, then, let it be buried.

Col: This is admirable black pudding: miss, shall I carve you some? I can just carve pudding, and that's all; I am the worst carver in the world; I should never make a good chaplain.

Miss: No thank ye, Colonel; for they say those that eat black pudding will dream of the devil.

Ld Smart. O, here comes the venison pasty: here, take the soup away.

Ld Smart [*he cuts it up, and tastes the venison*]: 'Sbuds, this venison is musty.

Neverout *eats a bit, and it burns his mouth*

Ld Smart: What's the matter, Tom? you have tears in your eyes, I think: what dost cry for, man?

Neverout: My lord, I was just thinking of my poor grandmother! she died just this very day seven years.

Miss *takes a bit and burns her mouth*

Neverout: And pray, miss, why do you cry, too?

Miss: Because you were not hanged the day your grandmother died.

Ld Smart: I'd have given forty pounds, miss, to have said that.

Col: Egad, I think the more I eat, the hungrier I am.

Ld Sparkish: Why, Colonel, they say one shoulder of mutton drives down another.

Neverout: Egad, if I were to fast for my life, I would take

a good breakfast in the morning, a good dinner at noon, and a good supper at night.

LD SPARKISH: My lord, this venison is plaguily peppered; your cook has a heavy hand.

LD SMART: My lord, I hope you are pepper-proof: come, here's a health to the founders.

LADY SMART: Ay; and to the confounders too.

LD SMART: Lady Answerall, does not your ladyship love venison?

LADY ANSW: No, my lord, I can't endure it in my sight: therefore please to send me a good piece of meat and crust.

LD SPARKISH [*drinks to* NEVEROUT]: Come, Tom; not always to my friends, but once to you.

NEVEROUT [*drinks to* LADY SMART]: Come, madam; here's a health to our friends and hang the rest of our kin.

LADY SMART [*to* LADY ANSW]: Madam, will your ladyship have any of this hare?

LADY ANSW: No, madam; they say, 'tis melancholy meat.

LADY SMART: Then, madam, shall I send you the brains? I beg your ladyship's pardon; for they say, 'tis not good manners to offer brains.

LADY ANSW: No, madam: for perhaps it will make me hare-brained.

NEVEROUT: Miss, I must tell you one thing.

MISS [*with a glass in her hand*]: Hold your tongue, Mr Neverout; don't speak in my tip.

COL: Well, he was an ingenious man that first found out eating and drinking.

LD SPARKISH: Of all victuals drink digests the quickest: give me a glass of wine.

NEVEROUT: My lord, your wine is too strong.

LD SMART: Ay, Tom, as much as you're too good.

MISS: This almond pudding was pure good; but it is grown quite cold.

NEVEROUT: So much the better, miss, cold pudding will settle your love.

MISS: Pray, Mr Neverout, are you going to take a voyage?

NEVEROUT: Why do you ask, miss?

MISS: Because you have laid in so much beef.

SIR JOHN: You two have eat up the whole pudding between you.

MISS: Sir John, here's a little bit left; will you please to have it?

SIR JOHN: No, thankee; I don't love to make a fool of my mouth.

COL [*calling to the butler*]: John, is your small beer good?

BUTLER: An please your honour, my lord and lady like it; I think it is good.

COL: Why then, John, d'ye see, if you are sure your small beer is good, d'ye mark? then, give me a glass of wine.

[*All laugh.*]

COLONEL *tasting the wine*

LD SMART: Sir John, how does your neighbour Gatherall, of the Peak? I hear he has lately made a purchase.

SIR JOHN: O! Dick Gatherall knows how to butter his bread as well as any man in Derbyshire.

LD SMART: Why he used to go very fine, when he was here in town.

SIR JOHN: Ay; and it became him as a saddle becomes a sow.

COL: I know his lady, and I think she is a very good woman.

SIR JOHN: 'Faith, she has more goodness in her little finger than he has in his whole body.

LD SMART: Well, Colonel, how do you like that wine?

COL: This wine should be eaten, it is too good to be drunk.

LD SMART: I'm very glad you like it; and pray don't spare it.

COL: No, my lord; I'll never starve in a cook's shop.

LD SMART: And pray, Sir John, what do you say to my wine?

SIR JOHN: I'll take another glass first: second thoughts are best.

LD SPARKISH: Pray, Lady Smart, you sit near that ham; will you please to send me a bit?

LADY SMART: With all my heart. [*She sends him piece.*] Pray, my lord, how do you like it?

LD SPARKISH: I think it is a limb of Lot's wife. [*He eats it with mustard.*] Egad, my lord, your mustard is very uncivil.

LADY SMART: Why uncivil, my lord?

LD SPARKISH: Because it takes me by the nose, egad.

LADY SMART: Mr Neverout, I find you are a very good carver.

COL: O madam, that is no wonder; for you must know, Tom Neverout carves o' Sundays.

NEVEROUT *overturns the salt cellar*

LADY SMART: Mr Neverout, you have overturned the salt, and that's a sign of anger: I'm afraid miss and you will fall out.

LADY ANSW: No, no; throw a little of it into the fire, and all will be well.

NEVEROUT: O, madam, the falling out of lovers, you know –

MISS: Lovers! very fine! fall out with him! I wonder when we were in.

SIR JOHN: For my part, I believe the young gentlewoman is his sweetheart, there is so much fooling and fiddling betwixt them; I'm sure, they say in our country, that shiddle-come shit's the beginning of love.

MISS: I own I love Mr Neverout as the devil loves holy water: I love him like pie, I'd rather the devil had him than I.

NEVEROUT: Miss, I'll tell you one thing.

MISS: Come, here's t'ye, to stop your mouth.

NEVEROUT: I'd rather you would stop it with a kiss.

MISS: A kiss! marry come up, my dirty cousin; are you no sicker? Lord! I wonder what fool it was that first invented kissing!

NEVEROUT: Well, I'm very dry.

MISS: Then you're the better to burn and the worse to fry.

LADY ANSW: God bless you, Colonel, you have a good stroke with you.

COL: O, madam, formerly I could eat all, but now I leave nothing; I eat but one meal a day.

MISS: What! I suppose, Colonel, that is from morning till night.

NEVEROUT: 'Faith, miss; and well was his wont.

LD SMART: Pray, Lady Answerall, taste this bit of venison.

LADY ANSW: I hope your lordship will set me a good example.

LD SMART: Here's a glass of cider filled: miss, you must drink it.

MISS: Indeed, my lord, I can't.

NEVEROUT: Come, miss; better belly burst, than good liquor be lost.

MISS: Pish! well in life there was never anything so teasing: I had rather shed it in my shoes: I wish it were in your guts, for my share.

LD SMART: Mr Neverout, you ha'nt tasted my cider yet.

NEVEROUT: No, my lord; I have been just eating soup; and they say, if one drinks with one's porridge, one will cough in one's grave.

LD SMART: Come, take miss's glass, she wished it was in your guts; let her have her wish for once: ladies can't abide to have their inclinations crossed.

LADY SMART [*to* SIR JOHN]: I think, Sir John, you have not tasted the venison yet.

SIR JOHN: I seldom eat it, madam; however, please to send me a little of the crust.

LD SPARKISH: Why, Sir John, you had as good eat the devil as the broth he is boiled in.

COL: Well, this eating and drinking takes away a body's stomach, as Lady Answerall says.

NEVEROUT: I have dined as well as my lord mayor.

MISS: I thought I could have eaten this wing of chicken; but my eye's bigger than my belly.

LD SMART: Indeed, Lady Answerall, you have eaten nothing.

LADY ANSW: Pray, my lord, see all the bones on my plate: they say a carpenter's known by his chips.

NEVEROUT: Miss, will you reach me that glass of jelly?

MISS [*giving it to him*]: You see, 'tis but ask and have.

NEVEROUT: Miss, I would have a bigger glass.

MISS: What? you don't know your own mind; you are neither well, full nor fasting: I think that is enough.

NEVEROUT: Ay, one of the enoughs; I am sure it is little enough.

MISS: Yes; but you know, sweet things are bad for the teeth.

NEVEROUT [*to* LADY ANSW]: Madam, I don't like that part of the veal you sent me.

LADY ANSW: Well, Mr Neverout, I find you are a true Englishman; you never know when you are well.

COL: Well, I have made my whole dinner of beef.

LADY ANSW: Why, Colonel, a bellyful's a bellyful, if it be but of wheat straw.

COL: Well, after all, kitchen physic is the best physic.

LADY SMART: And the best doctors in the world are doctor diet, doctor quiet, and doctor merryman.

LD SPARKISH: What do you think of a little house well filled?

SIR JOHN: And a little land well tilled?

COL: Ay; and a little wife well willed?

NEVEROUT: My Lady Smart, pray help me to some of the breast of that goose.

LD SMART: Tom, I have heard that goose upon goose is false heraldry.

MISS: What! will you never have done stuffing?

LD SMART: This goose is quite raw; well, God sends meat, but the devil sends cooks.

NEVEROUT: Miss, can you tell which is the gander, the white goose or the grey goose?

MISS: They say, a fool will ask more questions than the wisest body can answer.

COL: Indeed, miss, Tom Neverout has posed you.

MISS: Why, Colonel, every dog has his day; I believe I shall never see a goose again without thinking of Mr Neverout.

LD SMART: Well said, miss; 'faith, girl, thou hast brought thyself off cleverly. Tom, what say you to that?

COL: 'Faith, Tom is nonplussed: he looks plaguily down in the mouth.

MISS: Why, my lord, you see he is the provokingest creature in life; I believe there is not such another in the varsal[33] world.

LADY ANSW: O, miss, the world's a wide place.

NEVEROUT: Well, miss, I'll give you leave to call me anything, if you don't call me spade.

LD SMART: Well, but after all, Tom, can you tell me what's Latin for a goose?

NEVEROUT: O, my lord, I know that: why brandy is Latin for a goose, and *tace* is Latin for a candle.[34]

MISS: Is that manners, to show your learning before ladies? Methinks you are grown very brisk of a sudden; I think the man's glad he's alive.

SIR JOHN: The devil take your wit, if this be wit, for it spoils company: pray, Mr Butler, bring me a dram after my goose; 'tis very good for the wholesomes.

LD SMART: Come, bring me the loaf; I sometimes love to cut my own bread.

MISS: I suppose, my lord, you lay longest abed today.

LD SMART: Miss, if I had said so, I should have told a fib; I warrant you lay abed till the cows come home; but, miss, shall I cut you a little crust now my hand is in?

MISS: If you please, my lord, a bit of under-crust.

NEVEROUT [*whispering* MISS]: I find you love to lie under.

MISS [*aloud, pushing him from her*]: What does the man mean! Sir, I don't understand you at all.

NEVEROUT: Come, all quarrels laid aside: here, miss, may you live a thousand years.

[*He drinks to her.*]

MISS: Pray, sir, don't stint me.

LD SMART: Sir John, will you taste my October? I think it is very good: but I believe not equal to yours in Derbyshire.

SIR JOHN: My lord, I beg your pardon: but they say, the devil made askers.

LD SMART [*to the butler*]: Here, bring up the great tankard full of October for Sir John.

COL [*drinking to* MISS]: Miss, your health; may you live all the days of your life.

LADY ANSW: Well, miss, you'll certainly be soon married; here's two bachelors drinking to you at once.

LADY SMART: Indeed, miss, I believe you were wrapt in your mother's smock, you are so well beloved.

MISS: Where's my knife? sure I han't eaten it: O, here it is.

SIR JOHN: No, miss; but your maidenhead hangs in your light.

MISS: Pray, Sir John, is that a Derbyshire compliment? Here Mr Neverout, will you take this piece of rabbit that you bid me carve for you?

NEVEROUT: I don't know.

MISS: Why, take it or let it alone.

NEVEROUT: I will.

MISS: What will you?

NEVEROUT: Why, I'll take it, or let it alone.

MISS: You are a provoking creature.

SIR JOHN [*talking with a glass of wine in his hand*]: I remember a farmer in our country –

LD SMART [*interrupting him*]: Pray, Sir John, did you ever hear of parson Palmer?

SIR JOHN: No, my lord; what of him?

LD SMART: Why, he used to preach over his liquor.

SIR JOHN: I beg your lordship's pardon, here's your lordship's health; I'd drink it up, if it were a mile to the bottom.

LADY SMART: Mr Neverout, have you been at the new play?

NEVEROUT: Yes, madam, I went the first night.

LADY SMART: Well, and how did it take?

NEVEROUT: Why, madam, the poet is damned.

SIR JOHN: God forgive you! that's very uncharitable: you ought not to judge so rashly of any Christian.

NEVEROUT [*whispers* LADY SMART]: Was ever such a dunce! How well he knows the town! See how he stares like a stuck pig! Well, but Sir John, are you acquainted with any of our fine ladies yet?

SIR JOHN: No; damn your fire ships,[35] I have a wife of my own.

LADY SMART: Pray, my Lady Answerall, how do you like these preserved oranges?

LADY ANSW: Indeed, madam, the only fault I find is, that they are too good.

LADY SMART: O madam, I have heard 'em say, that too good is stark naught.

MISS *drinking part of a glass of wine*

NEVEROUT: Pray, let me drink your snuff.

MISS: No, indeed, you shan't drink after me; for you'll know my thoughts.

NEVEROUT: I know them already; you are thinking of a good husband. Besides, I can tell your meaning by your mumping.[36]

LADY SMART: Pray, my lord, did not you order the butler to bring up a tankard of our October to Sir John? I believe they stay to brew it.

The butler brings up the tankard to SIR JOHN

SIR JOHN: Won't your ladyship please to drink first?

LADY SMART: No, Sir John; 'tis in a very good hand; I'll pledge you.

COL [*to* LD SMART]: My Lord, I love October as well as Sir John; and I hope you won't make fish of one and flesh of another.

LD SMART: Colonel, you're heartily welcome. Come, Sir John, take it by word of mouth, and then give it the colonel.

SIR JOHN *drinks*

LADY SMART: Well, Sir John, how do you like it?

SIR JOHN: Not as well as my own in Derbyshire; 'tis plaguy small.

LADY SMART: I never taste malt liquor; but they say 'tis well hopped.

SIR JOHN: Hopped! why, if it had hopped a little further, it would have hopped into the river. Oh, my lord, my ale is meat, drink, and cloth; it will make a cat speak, and a wise man dumb.

LADY SMART: I was told ours was very strong.

SIR JOHN: Ay, madam, strong of the water; I believe the brewer forgot the malt, or the river was too near him. 'Faith, it is mere whip-belly vengeance;[37] he that drinks most has the worst share.

COL: I believe, Sir John, ale is as plenty as water at your house.

SIR JOHN: Why, 'faith, at Christmas we have many comers and goers: and they must not be set away without a cup of Christmas ale, for fear they should piss behind the door.

LADY SMART: I hear, Sir John has the nicest garden in England; they say, 'tis kept so clean, that you can't find a place where to spit.

SIR JOHN: Oh, madam; you are pleased to say so.

LADY SMART: But, Sir John, your ale is terrible strong and heady in Derbyshire, and will soon make one drunk and sick; what do you then?

SIR JOHN: Why, indeed, it is apt to fox one; but our way is, to take a hair of the same dog next morning. I take a new-laid egg for breakfast: and 'faith one should drink as much after an egg as after an ox.

LD SMART: Tom Neverout, will you taste a glass of October?

NEVEROUT: No, 'faith, my lord; I like your wine, and I won't put a churl upon a gentleman; your honour's claret is good enough for me.

LADY SMART: What! is this pigeon left for manners? Colonel, shall I send you the legs and rump?

COL: Madam, I could not eat a bit more, if the house was full.

LD SMART [*carving a partridge*]: Well: one may ride to Rumford upon this knife, it is so blunt.

LADY ANSW: My lord, I beg your pardon; but they say, an ill workman never had good tools.

LD SMART: Will your lordship have a wing of it?

LD SPARKISH: No, my lord; I love the wing of an ox a great deal better.

LD SMART: I'm always cold after eating.

COL: My lord, they say, that's a sign of long life.

LD SMART: Ay; I believe I shall live till all friends are weary of me.

COL: Pray, does anybody here hate cheese? I would be glad of a bit.

LD SMART: An odd kind of fellow dined with me t'other day; and when the cheese came upon the table, he pretended to faint: so somebody said, 'Pray take away the cheese': 'No,' said I, 'pray, take away the fool': said I well?

Here a loud and large laugh

COL: 'Faith, my lord, you served the coxcomb right enough: and therefore I wish we had a bit of your lordship's Oxfordshire cheese.

LD SMART: Come, hang saving; bring us up a halfp'orth of cheese.

LADY ANSW: They say, cheese digests everything but itself.

A footman brings a great whole cheese

LD SPARKISH: Ay; this would look handsome, if anybody should come in.

SIR JOHN: Well; I'm weily brosten,[38] as they say in Lancashire.

LD SMART: O! Sir John; I would I had something to brost you withal.

LADY SMART: Come, they say, 'tis merry in the hall when beards wag all.

LD SMART: Miss, shall I help you to some cheese, or will you carve for yourself?

NEVEROUT: I'll hold fifty pounds, miss won't cut the cheese.

MISS: Pray, why so, Mr Neverout?

NEVEROUT: O, there is a reason, and you know it well enough.

MISS: I can't for my life understand what the gentleman means.

LD SMART: Pray, Tom, change the discourse; in troth you are too bad.

COL [*whispers* NEVEROUT]: Smoke, miss; 'faith you have made her fret like gum taffeta.[39]

LADY SMART: Well, but, miss (hold your tongue, Mr Neverout), shall I cut you a piece of cheese?

MISS: No, really, madam; I have dined this half hour.

LADY SMART: What! quick at meat, quick at work, they say.

SIR JOHN *nods*

LD SMART: What! are you sleepy, Sir John? do you sleep after dinner?

SIR JOHN: Yes, 'faith; I sometimes take a nap after my pipe; for when the belly is full, the bones would be at rest.

LADY SMART: Come, Colonel; help yourself, and your friends will love you the better. [*To* LADY ANSW] Madam, your ladyship eats nothing.

LADY ANSW: Lord, madam, I have fed like a farmer, I shall grow as fat as a porpoise; I swear, my jaws are weary of chewing.

COL: I have a mind to eat a piece of that sturgeon, but fear it will make me sick.

NEVEROUT: A rare soldier indeed! let it alone, and I warrant it won't hurt you.

COL: Well, it would vex a dog to see a pudding creep.

SIR JOHN *rises*

LD SMART: Sir John, what are you doing?

SIR JOHN: Swolks,[40] I must be going, by'r lady; I have earnest business; I must do as the beggars do, go away when I have got enough.

LD SMART: Well; but stay till this bottle's out; you know, the man was hanged that left his liquor behind him; and besides, a cup in the pate is a mile in the gate; and a spur in the head is worth two in the heel.

SIR JOHN: Come, then; one brimmer to all your healths. [*The footman gives him a glass half full.*] Pray, friend, what was the rest of this glass made for? an inch at the top, friend, is worth two at the bottom. [*He gets a brimmer and drinks it off.*] Well, there's no deceit in a brimmer, and there's no false Latin in this; your wine is excellent good, so I thank you for the next, for I am sure of this; madam, has your ladyship any commands in Derbyshire? I must go fifteen miles tonight.

LADY SMART: None, Sir John, but to take care of yourself;

and my most humble service to your lady unknown.

SIR JOHN: Well, madam, I can but love and thank you.

LADY SMART: Here, bring water to wash; though really, you have all eaten so little that you have not need to wash your mouths.

LD SMART: But prithee, Sir John, stay a while longer.

SIR JOHN: No, my Lord; I am to smoke a pipe with a friend before I leave the town.

COL: Why, Sir John, had not you better set out tomorrow?

SIR JOHN: Colonel, you forget tomorrow is Sunday.

COL: Now I always love to begin a journey on Sundays, because I shall have the prayers of the church to preserve all that travel by land or by water.

SIR JOHN: Well, Colonel, thou are a mad fellow to make a priest of.

NEVEROUT: Fie, Sir John, do you take tobacco? How can you make a chimney of your mouth?

SIR JOHN [*to* NEVEROUT]: What! you don't smoke, I warrant you, but you smock. (Ladies, I beg your pardon.) Colonel, do you never smoke?

COL: No, Sir John; but I take a pipe sometimes.

SIR JOHN: I'faith, one of your finical London blades dined with me last year in Derbyshire: so, after dinner, I took a pipe; so, my gentleman turned away his head. So, said I, What, sir, do you never smoke? so, he answered as you do, Colonel; No, but I sometimes take a pipe: so he took a pipe in his hand, and fiddled with it till he broke it. So, said I, pray, sir, can you make a pipe? So he said, no. So, said I, Why then, sir, if you can't make a pipe, you should not break a pipe; so we all laughed.

LD SMART: Well, but Sir John, they say, that the corruption of pipes is the generation of stoppers.

SIR JOHN: Colonel, I hear you go sometimes to Derbyshire; I wish you would come and foul a plate with me.

COL: I hope you will give me a soldier's bottle.

SIR JOHN: Come and try. Mr Neverout, you are a town wit; can you tell me what kind of herb is tobacco?

NEVEROUT: Why, an Indian herb, Sir John.

SIR JOHN: No, 'tis a pot-herb; and so here's t'ye in a pot of my lord's October.

LADY SMART: I hear, Sir John, since you are married, you have forswore the town.

SIR JOHN: No, madam, I never forswore anything but the building of churches.

LADY SMART: Well, but Sir John, when may we hope to see you again in London?

SIR JOHN: Why, madam, not till the ducks have eat up the dirt, as the children say.

NEVEROUT: Come, Sir John, I foresee it will rain terribly.

LADY SMART: Come, Sir John, do nothing rashly; let us drink first.

LD SPARKISH: I know Sir John will go, though he was sure it would rain cats and dogs; but pray stay, Sir John: you'll be time enough to go to bed by candlelight.

LD SMART: Why, Sir John, if you must needs go, while you stay make use of your time. Here's my service to you, a health to our friend in Derbyshire. Come, sit down: let us put off the evil hour as long as we can.

SIR JOHN: 'Faith, I could not drink a drop more if the house was full.

COL: Why, Sir John, you used to love a glass of good wine in former times.

SIR JOHN: Why, so I do still, Colonel; but a man may love his house very well without riding the ridge:[41] besides, I must be with my wife on Tuesday, or there will be the devil and all to pay.

COL: Well, if you go today, I wish you may be wet to the skin.

SIR JOHN: Ay; but they say the prayers of the wicked won't prevail.

SIR JOHN *takes leave and goes away*

LD SMART: Well, miss, how do you like Sir John?

MISS: Why, I think he's a little upon the silly, or so: I believe he has not all the wit in the world: but I don't pretend to be a judge.

NEVEROUT: 'Faith, I believe, he was bred at Hog's Norton, where the pigs play upon the organs.

LD SPARKISH: Why, Tom, I thought you and he were hand and glove.

NEVEROUT: 'Faith, he shall have a clear threshold for me; I never darkened his door in my life, neither in town nor country; but he's a queer old duke, by my conscience; and yet after all I take him to be more knave than fool.

LADY SMART: Well, come, a man's a man, if he has but a nose on his face.

COL: I was once with him and some other company over a bottle; and, egad, he fell asleep, and snored so hard that we thought he was driving his hogs to market.

NEVEROUT: Why, what! you can have no more of a cat than her skin; you can't make a silk purse out of a sow's ear.

LD SPARKISH: Well, since he's gone, the devil go with him and sixpence; and there's money and company too.

NEVEROUT: 'Faith he's a true country put.[42] Pray, miss, let me ask you a question.

Miss: Well, but don't ask questions with a dirty face: I warrant what you have to say will keep cold.

Col: Come, my Lord, against you are disposed: here's to all that love and honour you.

Ld Sparkish: Ay, that was always Dick Nimble's health. I'm sure you know he's dead.

Col: Dead! well, my Lord, you love to be a messenger of ill news: I'm heartily sorry; but, my Lord, we must all die.

Neverout: I knew him very well; but pray, how came he to die?

Miss: There's a question! you talk like a poticary;[43] why, because he could live no longer.

Neverout: Well; rest his soul, we must live by the living, and not by the dead.

Ld Sparkish: You know, his house was burnt down to the ground.

Col: Yes; it was in the news. Why, fire and water are good servants, but they are very bad masters.

Ld Smart: Here, take away, and set down a bottle of burgundy. Ladies, you'll stay and drink a glass of wine before you go to your tea?

All taken away, and the wine set down, etc.
Miss *gives* Neverout *a smart pinch*

Neverout: Lord, miss, what d'ye mean? d'ye think I have no feeling?

Miss: I'm forced to pinch, for the times are hard.

Neverout [*giving* Miss *a pinch*]: Take that, miss; what's sauce for a goose is sauce for a gander.

Miss [*screaming*]: Well, Mr Neverout, that shall neither go to Heaven nor Hell with you.

Neverout [*takes* Miss *by the hand*]: Come, miss, let us lay quarrels aside, and be friends.

Miss: Don't be so teasing; you plague a body so! can't you keep your filthy hands to yourself?

Neverout: Pray, miss, where did you get that pick-tooth case?

Miss: I came honestly by it.

Neverout: I'm sure it was mine, for I lost just such a one; nay, I don't tell you a lie.

Miss: No; if you lie it is much.

Neverout: Well, I'm sure 'tis mine.

Miss: What! you think everything is yours, but a little the king has.

Neverout: Colonel, you have seen my fine pick-tooth case; don't you think this is the very same?

Col: Indeed, miss, it is very like it.

Miss: Ay, what he says, you'll swear.

Neverout: Well, but I'll prove it to be mine.

Miss: Ay, do if you can.

Neverout: Why, what's yours is mine, and what's mine is my own.

Miss: Well, run on till you're weary; nobody holds you.

Neverout *gapes*

Col: What, Mr Neverout, do you gape for preferment?

Neverout: 'Faith, I may gape long enough before it falls into my mouth.

Lady Smart: Mr Neverout, my lord and I intend to beat up your quarters one of these days: I hear you live high.

Neverout: Yes, 'faith, madam, I live high, and lodge in a garret.

COL: But, miss, I forgot to tell you that Mr Neverout got the devilishest fall in the Park today.

MISS: I hope he did not hurt the ground: but how was it, Mr Neverout? I wish I had been there to laugh.

NEVEROUT: Why, madam, it was a place where a cuckold had been buried, and one of his horns sticking out, I happened to stumble against it; that was all.

LADY SMART: Ladies, let us leave the gentlemen to themselves; I think it is time to go to our tea.

LADY ANSW *and* MISS: My lords and gentlemen, your most humble servant.

LD SMART: Well, ladies, we'll wait on you an hour hence.

The gentlemen alone

LD SMART: Come, John, bring us a fresh bottle.

COL: Ay, my lord; and pray let him carry off the dead men, as we say in the army.

> [*Meaning the empty bottles.*]

LD SPARKISH: Mr Neverout, pray is not that bottle full?

NEVEROUT: Yes, my Lord; full of emptiness.

LD SMART: And, d'ye hear, John, bring clean glasses.

COL: I'll keep mine; for I think wine is the best liquor to wash glasses in.

DIALOGUE III

The ladies at their tea

LADY SMART: Well, ladies; now let us have a cup of discourse to ourselves.

LADY ANSW: What do you think of your friend, Sir John Spendall?

LADY SMART: Why, madam, 'tis happy for him that his father was born before him.

MISS: They say he makes a very ill husband to my lady.

LADY ANSW: But he must be allowed to be the fondest father in the world.

LADY SMART: Ay, madam, that's true; for they say the devil is kind to his own.

MISS: I am told, my lady manages him to admiration.

LADY SMART: That I believe, for she's as cunning as a dead pig, but not half so honest.

LADY ANSW: They say, she's quite a stranger to all his gallantries.

LADY SMART: Not at all; but you know there's none so blind as they that won't see.

MISS: Oh, madam, I am told she watches him as a cat would watch a mouse.

LADY ANSW: Well, if she ben't foully belied, she pays him in his own coin.

LADY SMART: Madam, I fancy I know your thoughts, as well as if I were within you.

LADY ANSW: Madam, I was t'other day in company with Mrs Clatter; I find she gives herself airs of being acquainted with your ladyship.

MISS: Oh! the hideous creature! did you observe her nails?

they were long enough to scratch her grannam out of her grave.

LADY SMART: Well, she and Tom Gosling were banging compliments backward and forward: it looked like two asses scrubbing one another.

MISS: Ay, claw me, and I'll claw you: but pray, madam, who were the company?

LADY SMART: Why, there was all the world, and his wife; there was Mrs Clatter, Lady Singular, the Countess of Talkham (I should have named her first), Tom Gosling, and some others, whom I have forgot.

LADY ANSW: I think the countess is very sickly.

LADY SMART: Yes, madam; she'll never scratch a grey head, I promise her.

MISS: And pray, what was your conversation?

LADY SMART: Why, Mrs Clatter had all the talk to herself, and was perpetually complaining of her misfortunes.

LADY ANSW: She brought her husband ten thousand pounds; she has a town house and country house: would the woman have her arse hung with points?

LADY SMART: She would fain be at the top of the house before the stairs are built.

MISS: Well, comparisons are odious; but she's as like her husband as if she were spit out of his mouth; as like as one egg is to another. Pray how was she drest?

LADY SMART: Why, she was as fine as fi'pence; but, truly, I thought there was more cost than worship.

LADY ANSW: I don't know her husband: pray, what is he?

LADY SMART: Why, he's a counsellor of the law; you must know he came to us as drunk as David's sow.[44]

MISS: What kind of creature is he?

LADY SMART: You must know the man and his wife are

coupled like rabbits, a fat and a lean; he's as fat as a
porpoise, and she's one of Pharaoh's lean kine: the ladies
and Tom Gosling were proposing a party at quadrille,
but he refused to make one. Damn your cards, said he,
they are the devil's books.

Lady Answ: A dull, unmannerly brute! well, God send him
more wit, and me more money.

Miss: Lord! madam, I would not keep such company for
the world.

Lady Smart: Oh, miss, 'tis nothing when you are used to it:
besides, you know, for want of company, welcome trumpery.

Miss: Did your ladyship play?

Lady Smart: Yes, and won; so I came off with fiddler's fare,
meat, drink, and money.

Lady Answ: Ay; what says Pluck?[45]

Miss: Well, my elbow itches; I shall change bedfellows.

Lady Smart: And my right hand itches; I shall receive money.

Lady Answ: And my right eye itches; I shall cry.

Lady Smart: Miss, I hear your friend Mistress Giddy has
discarded Dick Shuttle: pray, has she got another lover?

Miss: I hear of none.

Lady Smart: Why, the fellow's rich, and I think she was
a fool to throw out her dirty water before she got clean.

Lady Answ: Miss, that's a very handsome gown of yours,
and finely made; very genteel.

Miss: I am glad your ladyship likes it.

Lady Answ: Your lover will be in raptures; it becomes you
admirably.

Miss: Ay; I assure you I won't take it as I have done; if this
won't fetch him, the devil fetch him, say I.

Lady Smart [*to* Lady Answ]: Pray, madam, when did you
see Sir Peter Muckworm?

LADY ANSW: Not this fortnight; I hear he's laid up with the gout.

LADY SMART: What does he do for it?

LADY ANSW: I hear he's weary of doctoring it, and now makes use of nothing but patience and flannel.

MISS: Pray, how does he and my lady agree?

LADY ANSW: You know he loves her as the devil loves holy water.

MISS: They say, she plays deep with sharpers, that cheat her of her money.

LADY ANSW: Upon my word, they must rise early that would cheat her of her money; sharp's the word with her; diamonds cut diamonds.

MISS: Well, but I was assured from a good hand, that she lost at one sitting to the tune of a hundred guineas; make money of that!

LADY SMART: Well, but do you hear that Mrs Plump is brought to bed at last?

MISS: And pray, what has God sent her?

LADY SMART: Why, guess if you can.

MISS: A boy, I suppose.

LADY SMART: No, you are out; guess again.

MISS: A girl, then.

LADY SMART: You have hit it; I believe you are a witch.

MISS: O madam, the gentlemen say, all fine ladies are witches; but I pretend to no such thing.

LADY ANSW: Well, she had good luck to draw Tom Plump into wedlock; she ris' with her arse upwards.

MISS: Fie, madam; what do you mean?

LADY SMART: O miss, 'tis nothing what we say among ourselves.

MISS: Ay, madam; but they say, hedges have eyes, and walls

have ears.

LADY ANSW: Well, miss, I can't help it; you know I'm old Telltruth; I love to call a spade a spade.

LADY SMART [*mistakes the tea-tongs for the spoon*]: What! I think my wits are a wool-gathering today.

MISS: Why, madam, there was but a right and a wrong.

LADY SMART: Miss, I hear that you and Lady Coupler are as great as cup and can.

LADY ANSW: Ay, miss, as great as the devil and the Earl of Kent.

LADY SMART: Nay, I am told you meet together with as much love as there is between the old cow and the haystack.

MISS: I own I love her very well; but there's difference between staring and stark mad.

LADY SMART: They say, she begins to grow it.

MISS: Fat! ay, fat as a hen in the forehead.

LADY SMART: Indeed, Lady Answerall (pray forgive me), I think your ladyship looks thinner than when I saw you last.

MISS: Indeed, madam, I think not; but your ladyship is one of Job's comforters.

LADY ANSW: Well, no matter how I look; I am bought and sold; but really, miss, you are so very obliging, that I wish I were a handsome young lord for your sake.

MISS: O, madam, your love's a million.

LADY SMART [*to* LADY ANSW]: Madam, will your ladyship let me wait on you to the play tomorrow?

LADY ANSW: Madam, it becomes me to wait on your ladyship.

MISS: What, then, I'm turned out for a wrangler?

The gentlemen come in to the ladies to drink tea

MISS: Mr Neverout, we wanted you sadly; you are always out of the way when you should be hanged.

NEVEROUT: You wanted me! pray, miss, how do you look when you lie?

MISS: Better than you when you cry. Manners indeed! I find you mend like sour ale in summer.

NEVEROUT: I beg your pardon, miss; I only meant, when you lie alone.

MISS: That's well turned; one turn more would have turned you downstairs.

NEVEROUT: Come, miss, be kind for once, and order me a dish of coffee.

MISS: Pray, go yourself; let us wear out the oldest; besides, I can't go, for I have a bone in my leg.

COL: They say, a woman need but look on her apron string to find an excuse.

NEVEROUT: Why, miss, you are grown so peevish, a dog would not live with you.

MISS: Mr Nevcrout, I beg your diversion, no offence, I hope; but truly in a little time you intend to make the colonel as bad as yourself; and that's as bad as can be.

NEVEROUT: My lord, don't you think miss improves wonderfully of late? why, miss, if I spoil the colonel, I hope you will use him as you do me; for you know, love me, love my dog.

COL: How's that, Tom? Say that again: why, if I am a dog, shake hands, brother.

Here a great, loud, long laugh

LD SMART: But pray, gentlemen, why always so severe upon poor miss? on my conscience, Colonel and Tom Neverout, one of you two are both knaves.

COL: My Lady Answerall, I intend to do myself the honour of dining with your ladyship tomorrow.

LADY ANSW: Ay, Colonel, do if you can.

MISS: I'm sure you'll be glad to be welcome.

COL: Miss, I thank you; and to reward you, I'll come and drink tea with you in the morning.

MISS: Colonel, there's two words to that bargain.

COL [*to* LADY SMART]: Your ladyship has a very fine watch; well may you wear it.

LADY SMART: It is none of mine, Colonel.

COL: Pray, whose is it then?

LADY SMART: Why, 'tis my lord's; for they say a married woman has nothing of her own, but her wedding ring and her hair lace; but if women had been the law makers it would have been better.

COL: This watch seems to be quite new.

LADY SMART: No, sir, it has been twenty years in my lord's family; but Quare[46] put a new case and dial-plate to it.

NEVEROUT: Why, that's for all the world like the man who swore he kept the same knife forty years, only he sometimes changed the haft, and sometimes the blade.

LD SMART: Well, Tom, to give the devil his due, thou art a right woman's man.

COL: Odd so! I have broke the hinge of my snuff box; I'm undone, beside the loss.

MISS: Alack-a-day, Colonel! I vow I had rather have found forty shillings.

NEVEROUT: Why, Colonel, all that I can say to comfort you is, that you must mend it with a new one.

MISS *laughs*

COL: What, miss! you can't laugh but you must show your teeth.

MISS: I'm sure you show your teeth when you can't bite; well, thus it must be if we sell ale.

NEVEROUT: Miss, you smell very sweet; I hope you don't carry perfumes.

MISS: Perfumes! No, sir; I'd have you to know, it is nothing but the grain of my skin.

COL: Tom, you have a good nose to make a poor man's sow.

LD SPARKISH: So, ladies and gentlemen, methinks you are very witty upon one another; come box it about; 'twill come to my father at last.

COL: Why, my lord, you see miss has no mercy; I wish she were married; but I doubt the grey mare would prove the better horse.

MISS: Well, God forgive you for that wish.

LD SPARKISH: Never fear him, miss.

MISS: What, my lord, do you think I was born in a wood to be afraid of an owl?

LD SMART: What have you to say to that, Colonel?

NEVEROUT: Oh, my lord, my friend the colonel scorns to set his wit against a child.

MISS: Scornful dogs will eat dirty puddings.

COL: Well, miss, they say a woman's tongue is the last thing about her that dies; therefore let's kiss and be friends.

MISS: Hands off! that's meat for your master.

LD SPARKISH: 'Faith, Colonel, you are for ale and cakes: but after all, miss, you are too severe; you would not meddle with your match.

MISS: All they can say goes in at one ear, and out at t'other for me, I can assure you; only I wish they would be quiet, and let me drink my tea.

NEVEROUT: What! I warrant you think all is lost that goes
beside your own mouth.

MISS: Pray, Mr Neverout, hold your tongue for once, if it be
possible; one would think you were a woman in man's
clothes by your prating.

NEVEROUT: No, miss; it is not handsome to see one hold
one's tongue; besides I should slobber my fingers.

COL: Miss, did you never hear that three women and a goose
are enough to make a market?

MISS: I'm sure, if Mr Neverout or you were among them,
it would make a fair.

Footman comes in

LADY SMART: Here, take away the tea-table, and bring up
candles.

LADY ANSW: O madam, no candles yet, I beseech you; don't
let us burn daylight.

NEVEROUT: I dare swear, miss for her part will never burn
daylight, if she can help it.

MISS: Lord, Mr Neverout, one can't hear one's own ears
for you.

LADY SMART: Indeed, madam, it is blindman's holiday;[47]
we shall soon be all of a colour.

NEVEROUT: Why then, miss, we may kiss where we like best.

MISS: Fogh! these men talk of nothing but kissing.

[*She spits.*]

NEVEROUT: What, miss, does it make your mouth water?

LADY SMART: It is as good be in the dark as without light;
therefore, pray bring in candles; they say women and linen
show best by candlelight; come, gentlemen, are you for
a party at quadrille?

Col: I'll make one with you three ladies.

Lady Answ: I'll sit down and be a stander-by.

Lady Smart [*to* Lady Answ]: Madam, does your ladyship never play?

Col: Yes, I suppose her ladyship plays sometimes for an egg at Easter.

Neverout: Ay, and a kiss at Christmas.

Lady Answ: Come, Mr Neverout, hold your tongue, and mind your knitting.

Neverout: With all my heart; kiss my wife and welcome.

The Colonel, Mr Neverout, Lady Smart,
and Miss, *go to quadrille, and sit there
till three in the morning. They rise from cards*

Lady Smart: Well, miss, you'll have a sad husband, you have such good luck at cards.

Neverout: Indeed, miss, you dealt me sad cards; if you deal so ill by your friends, what will you do with your enemies?

Lady Answ: I'm sure 'tis time for honest folks to be a-bed.

Miss: Indeed my eyes draw straws.[48]

She's almost asleep

Neverout: Why, miss, if you fall asleep, somebody may get a pair of gloves.

Col: I'm going to the land of Nod.

Neverout: 'Faith, I'm for Bedfordshire.

Lady Smart: I'm sure I shall sleep without rocking.

Neverout: Miss, I hope you'll dream of your sweetheart.

Miss: Oh, no doubt of it; I believe I shan't be able to sleep for dreaming of him.

Col [*to* Miss]: Madam, shall I have the honour to escort you?

Miss: So, Colonel, I thank you; my mamma has sent her chair and footmen. Well, my Lady Smart, I'll give you revenge whenever you please.

Footman comes in

Footman: Madam, the chairs are waiting.

They all take their chairs and go off

NOTES

1. William III, known as William of Orange (1650–1702), King of Great Britain 1689–1702.

2. Charles II (1630–85), King of Britain and Ireland 1660–85, the son of Charles I.

3. Colonel James Graham (1649–1730). Under Queen Anne and George I, Colonel Graham was MP for Appleby and Westmorland.

4. Gilbert Burnet (1643–1715), English bishop and historian.

5. To sell someone a bargain is to make a fool of them in conversation.

6. Probably Swift's own couplet.

7. Sir John Perrot (c.1527–92), Lord Deputy of Ireland under Queen Elizabeth I and the reputed illegitimate son of Henry VIII.

8. William Lilly (1468–1522) was a grammarian and author of the most widely used Latin grammar in England.

9. Thomas Brown (1663–1704), translator and satirist.

10. Swift's mention of writers in the following passages is ironic, so that those he had little time for become 'eminent', while those that were his friends are 'that snarling brood'. Charles Gildon (1665–1724), miscellanist and hack; Ned Ward (1667–1731), miscellanist and humourist; John Dennis (1657–1734), critic.

11. John Ozell (d.1743), translator; Captain John Stevens (d.1726), translator and scholar.

12. Friends of Swift's: Alexander Pope (1688–1744), satirical poet; John Gay (1685–1732), writer, best known for his play *The Beggar's Opera*; John Arbuthnot (1667–1735), physician and satirical writer; Edward Young (1683–1765), poet.

13. Reference to the political periodical of the same name, to which Swift often contributed.

14. Lewis Theobald (1688–1744), literary hack and Shakespearean editor.

15. Colley Cibber (1671–1757), playwright.

16. One of these days, some time or another.

17. Verdict, opinion.

18. In prison.

19. The *1811 Dictionary of the Vulgar Tongue* has this definition: 'He must go to Battersea, to be cut for the simples – Battersea is a place famous for its garden grounds, some of which were formerly appropriated to the growing of simples for apothecaries, who at a certain season used to go down to select their stock for the ensuing year, at which time the gardeners were said to cut their simples; whence it became a popular joke to advise young people to go to Battersea, at that time, to have their simples cut, or to be cut for the simples.'

20. A game played with dice, probably so named from the silence observed when playing it.

21. 'Mapstick' is a corruption of 'mopstick' – the handle of a mop – and the phrase is probably a version of 'I cry you mercy'.

22. Slang for someone who is simple.

23. An abbreviation of "sbodikins' – God's bodikins (i.e. nails).

24. Said of someone who laughs without any apparent cause.

25. Low-spirited with an imaginary sickness, or perhaps stomach-ache.

26. 'The favourite or smallest pig in the litter. – To follow like a tantony pig, i.e. St Anthony's pig; to follow close at one's heels. St Anthony the hermit was a swineherd, and is always represented with a swine's bell and a pig. Some derive this saying from a privilege enjoyed by the friars of certain convents in England and France (sons of St Anthony), whose swine were permitted to feed in the streets. These swine would follow any one having greens or other provisions, till they obtained some of them; and it was in those days considered an act of charity and religion to feed them.' (*Dictionary of the Vulgar Tongue*)

27. Skeleton.

28. Someone often quarrelled with.

29. A sixpence.

30. 'Understumble… humblecumdumble'. In his notes to *Polite Conversation* (Andre Deutsch: London, 1963) Eric Partridge identifies 'understumble' as 'understand', and 'humblecumdumble' as 'humble servant', suggesting that Neverout is responding to Miss Notable with a sort of internal crambo.

31. 'Supposed to be a very brotherly set of people; "as great as two inkle weavers" being a proverbial saying.' (*Dictionary of the Vulgar Tongue*)

32. 'An affected or conceited coxcomb.' (*Dictionary of the Vulgar Tongue*)

33. Universal, whole.

34. 'Brandy is Latin for a goose; a memento to prevent the animal from rising in the stomach by a glass of the good creature'; 'Silence, hold your tongue. TACE is Latin for a candle; a jocular admonition to be silent on any subject.' (*Dictionary of the Vulgar Tongue*). Brewer's 1898 *Dictionary of Phrase and Fable* offers this explanation for 'Latin for a goose': 'Here is a pun between *anser,* a goose, and *answer,* to reply. What is the Latin for goose? Answer [*anser*] brandy.'

35. 'A wench who has the venereal disease.' (*Dictionary of the Vulgar Tongue*)

36. Grimacing.

37. 'Whip-belly vengeance or pinch-gut vengeance, of which he that gets the most has the worst share. Weak or sour beer.' (*Dictionary of the Vulgar Tongue*)

38. Well-nigh burst (dialect).

39. '*He frets like gummed velvet* or *gummed taffety.* Velvet and taffeta were sometimes stiffened with gum to make them "sit better," but, being very stiff, they fretted out quickly.' (*Dictionary of Phrase and Fable*)

40. Probably a corruption of "swounds' – God's wounds.

41. The ridge of the house – ie. a man may love something without resorting to grandiose gestures.

42. 'A country put; an ignorant awkward clown.' (*Dictionary of the Vulgar Tongue*)

43. Apothecary.

44. 'As drunk as David's sow; a common saying, which took its rise from the following circumstance: One David Lloyd, a Welchman, who kept an alehouse at Hereford, had a living sow with six legs, which was greatly resorted to by the curious; he had also a wife much addicted to drunkenness, for which he used sometimes to give her due correction. One day David's wife having taken a cup too much, and being fearful of the consequences, turned out the sow, and lay down to sleep herself sober in the stye. A company coming in to see the sow, David ushered them into the stye, exclaiming, there is a sow for you! did any of you ever see such another? all the while supposing the sow had really been there; to which some of the company, seeing the state the woman was in, replied, it was the drunkenest sow they had ever beheld; whence the woman was ever after called David's sow.' (*Dictionary of the Vulgar Tongue*)

45. 'What says Pluck?… I shall cry' – this reference is obscure, but Partridge suggests that these ailments and their interpretations were contemporary folklore.

46. Daniel Quare (1649–1724), celebrated maker of watches and clocks.

47. 'Night, darkness.' (*Dictionary of the Vulgar Tongue*)

48. 'His eyes draw straw; his eyes are almost shut, or he is almost asleep.' (*Dictionary of the Vulgar Tongue*)

Jonathan Swift was born in Dublin in 1667, into an Anglo–Irish Protestant family. His father died before Swift was born and his mother returned to her own family in England, leaving her son in the care of relatives. Swift received a good education in Kilkenny and later at Trinity College, Dublin.

After completing his degree, Swift moved for the first time to England, and, in 1689, he became secretary to Sir William Temple at Moor Park in Surrey. Here he met and fell in love with Esther Johnson, the 'Stella' of his journal. He visited Ireland briefly in 1690, but returned to England the following year, where he was awarded a degree from Oxford University in 1692. At about this time, Swift published his first poem; it did not meet with critical acclaim and his attempts to achieve a position in the Church in England were likewise unsuccessful, and in 1694 he returned once again to Ireland.

In 1695, Swift was finally ordained as an Anglican priest and given the small prebendary of Kilroot. He remained there for less than a year, however, and in 1696 returned to Moor Park. Here he began to write some of his greatest works, including the religious satire *A Tale of a Tub* and *The Battle of the Books*, a satire defending the works of the 'Ancients' against that of the 'Moderns'; both remained unpublished until 1704. In 1699 Temple died, and again Swift returned to Ireland, where he was appointed vicar of Laracor.

Swift continued to visit England, and became involved with Whig politics, writing several political pamphlets. His loyalties shifted, however, in 1707, when the Whigs dismissed his request for a remission of Irish clerical taxation, and in 1710 he became editor of the Tory newspaper *The Examiner*.

Swift became a founder member of the Scriblerus Club in 1714, a satirical literary group whose members also included John Arbuthnot, Alexander Pope, John Gay and Thomas Parnell, and whose influence was significant in Swift's own later work. Later the same year, however, the Tories fell from power and Swift was forced to return to Ireland for good, where he was installed as Dean of St Patrick's Cathedral in Dublin. He continued to produce satires and pamphlets, and rose to become a heroic figure in his native land with works such as *Drapier's Letters* (1724), protesting about English monopolies, and *A Modest Proposal* (1729), a savagely ironic work in which he suggested that the problem of the Irish famine could be solved if the Irish resorted to eating their own children.

Swift's most famous work, *Gulliver's Travels*, was published in 1726. It was a hugely successful social satire, although now largely regarded as a children's book, and demonstrated his intense and growing pessimism at what he perceived as the follies of mankind. His final years were filled with illness and bitterness; his mental state was almost certainly deteriorating from the 1730s onwards, and, in 1742, he suffered a stroke that left him in need of permanent care. In 1745, Swift died and was buried in St Patrick's Cathedral.

SELECTED TITLES FROM HESPERUS PRESS

Joseph Conrad	*Heart of Darkness*	A.N. Wilson
Joseph Conrad	*The Return*	Colm Tóibín
James Fenimore Cooper	*Autobiography of a Pocket Handkerchief*	Ruth Scurr
Dante Alighieri	*New Life*	Louis de Bernières
Dante Alighieri	*The Divine Comedy: Inferno*	Ian Thomson
Daniel Defoe	*The King of Pirates*	Peter Ackroyd
Charles Dickens	*The Haunted House*	Peter Ackroyd
Charles Dickens	*A House to Let*	
Charles Dickens	*Mrs Lirriper*	Philip Hensher
Charles Dickens	*Mugby Junction*	Robert Macfarlane
Charles Dickens	*The Wreck of the Golden Mary*	Simon Callow
Emily Dickinson	*The Single Hound*	Andrew Motion
Fyodor Dostoevsky	*The Double*	Jeremy Dyson
Fyodor Dostoevsky	*The Gambler*	Jonathan Franzen
Fyodor Dostoevsky	*Notes from the Underground*	Will Self
Fyodor Dostoevsky	*Poor People*	Charlotte Hobson
Arthur Conan Doyle	*The Mystery of Cloomber*	
Arthur Conan Doyle	*The Tragedy of the Korosko*	Tony Robinson
Alexandre Dumas	*Captain Pamphile*	Tony Robinson
Alexandre Dumas	*One Thousand and One Ghosts*	
Joseph von Eichendorff	*Life of a Good-for-nothing*	
George Eliot	*Amos Barton*	Matthew Sweet
George Eliot	*Mr Gilfil's Love Story*	Kirsty Gunn
J. Meade Falkner	*The Lost Stradivarius*	Tom Paulin
Henry Fielding	*Jonathan Wild the Great*	Peter Ackroyd
Gustave Flaubert	*Memoirs of a Madman*	Germaine Greer
Gustave Flaubert	*November*	Nadine Gordimer
E.M. Forster	*Arctic Summer*	Anita Desai

Prosper Mérimée	*Carmen*	Philip Pullman
Sir Thomas More	*The History of Richard III*	Sister Wendy Beckett
Sándor Petofi	*John the Valiant*	George Szirtes
Francis Petrarch	*My Secret Book*	Germaine Greer
Edgar Allan Poe	*Eureka*	Sir Patrick Moore
Alexander Pope	*Scriblerus*	Peter Ackroyd
Alexander Pope	*The Rape of the Lock and A Key to the Lock*	Peter Ackroyd
Antoine François Prévost	*Manon Lescaut*	Germaine Greer
Marcel Proust	*Pleasures and Days*	A.N. Wilson
Alexander Pushkin	*Dubrovsky*	Patrick Neate
Alexander Pushkin	*Ruslan and Lyudmila*	Colm Tóibín
François Rabelais	*Gargantua*	Paul Bailey
François Rabelais	*Pantagruel*	Paul Bailey
Christina Rossetti	*Commonplace*	Andrew Motion
Marquis de Sade	*Betrayal*	John Burnside
Marquis de Sade	*Incest*	Janet Street-Porter
Saki	*A Shot in the Dark*	Jeremy Dyson
George Sand	*The Devil's Pool*	Victoria Glendinning
Friedrich von Schiller	*The Ghost-seer*	Martin Jarvis
Mary Shelley	*Transformation*	
Percy Bysshe Shelley	*Zastrozzi*	Germaine Greer
Stendhal	*Memoirs of an Egotist*	Doris Lessing
Robert Louis Stevenson	*Dr Jekyll and Mr Hyde*	Helen Dunmore
Theodor Storm	*The Lake of the Bees*	Alan Sillitoe
Italo Svevo	*A Perfect Hoax*	Tim Parks
Jonathan Swift	*Directions to Servants*	Colm Tóibín
W.M. Thackeray	*Rebecca and Rowena*	Matthew Sweet
Leo Tolstoy	*The Death of Ivan Ilyich*	Nadine Gordimer
Leo Tolstoy	*The Forged Coupon*	Andrew Miller
Leo Tolstoy	*Hadji Murat*	Colm Tóibín

Ivan Turgenev	*Faust*	Simon Callow
Mark Twain	*The Diary of Adam and Eve*	John Updike
Mark Twain	*Tom Sawyer, Detective*	
Jules Verne	*A Fantasy of Dr Ox*	Gilbert Adair
Edith Wharton	*Sanctuary*	William Fiennes
Edith Wharton	*The Touchstone*	Salley Vickers
Oscar Wilde	*The Portrait of Mr W.H.*	Peter Ackroyd
Virginia Woolf	*Carlyle's House and Other Sketches*	Doris Lessing
Virginia Woolf	*Monday or Tuesday*	Scarlett Thomas
Virginia Woolf, Vanessa Bell with Thoby Stephen	*Hyde Park Gate News*	Hermione Lee
Emile Zola	*The Dream*	Tim Parks
Emile Zola	*For a Night of Love*	A.N. Wilson